# Come Again
# No More

# Come Again No More

A novel

David Wesley Williams

JACKLEG PRESS

JackLeg Press
www.jacklegpress.org

davidwesleywilliams.wordpress.com



ISBN: 978-1956907193



Library of Congress Control Number: 2023945766

Also by David Wesley Williams

*Everybody Knows* (JackLeg Press, 2023)
*Long Gone Daddies* (John F. Blair, Publisher, 2013)

For Barb. Some forty years ago she looked from her copy-desk perch across the newsroom of the *York Daily Record*, and saw a timid, young reporter just in for a job tryout. She thought, quite daftly, *I'm going to marry him.* And the next year, she did. To daft thoughts. To love. And to the business that brought us together.

To my newspaper colleagues over three states and four decades. We thought we'd change the world. We thought it would last forever. What were we thinking?

# The other f-word

And then we had the wake. It was lovely with tears and laughter, roar and uproar. Nobody died. Well, only a little. We all died a little. But death mostly let us be. Death seemed to think there was, for us, a fate worse than it. Which left us alive in the end, and so very, very drunk.

I remember parts of it. I remember it began with a benediction of sorts. It was Vollintine, the city editor, who gave it. He said he was the strayed son of an Irish Catholic father and a Hard-Shell Baptist mother and married a Pentecostal-raised dabbler in every religion from Neopaganism to Ghost Dance to Elvis Presley. So he had, he said, as much religion as any bastard or wench in the room. You would have thought a bastard was the very thing to be and a wench a rare and beautiful thing to glimpse in nature, like a blue-crested something, the way he said it. We all cheered, we bastards, we wenches. Vollintine carried on—or rather, he got started.

"We gather here, you mourners and we mourned, in this bar called Little Blind's, down on old South Main, in this city on the bluff, Memphis, Tennessee, on this Friday night, the eleventh day of May, in the Year of Ought Not …"

That's as far as he got, or as far as I remember him getting. I think he called for a drink then. Maybe he was shouted down. Or else that was all the benediction he intended to give, or that we required or deserved. The wake was on.

✳

I remember elegies and requiems. I remember toasts and chants. I remember blues songs about the midnight crawl and the dead rat swing. I remember someone, it may have been Flippen, who covered city hall, produced an actual dead rat. He paraded it through the bar, holding it by the tail and addressing it as our esteemed editor-in-chief. Most everyone remarked upon the likeness of rodent to man, though several allowed as how the rat was a slightly more handsome fellow and carried just less of a stench, and far fewer diseases. We cursed the editor in effigy and then we drank some more to our fates and then we broke into old stories about the time when …

✳

I'd forgotten how many rounds of layoffs there'd been. They'd been going on for a few years now. Reductions in Force, they called them. RIFs, for short, like some brand of kids' sneakers or a cartoon dog that spoke. You were riffed, and then you were riffraff. Pity, too, the ones who remained and tried to carry on. The newsroom was a third of its former size, a shell of itself, skeletal remains.

There were ten of us this time. Seven bastards, two wenches, and the poor son of a bitch who tells this tale.

Death by paper cut, the official cause.

✳

"But God forbid they'd say the word," I said.

"What word's that, Charley?"

I was sitting at the bar, two beers into the wake. It was Francis the bartender. Saint Francis, we called him. Patron Saint of the Pour. He slid another pint glass across the bar to me. Rim of foam at the lip. Perfection. He knew what I was about to say. He waited for me to say it. He knew I needed to.

"Fired," I said.

"Sure. Fired, of course, Charley. The other f-word."

"I made a scene of myself, Francis. I banged the table. I did everything but beg. I may have begged. But he wouldn't say the fucking word."

"The editor-in-chief, you mean."

"He said it wasn't the term they use. I said we don't use *terms*. We're newspaper people. We say things, straight out. We don't flinch. When some poor son of a bitch dies, we don't say he passed. We don't say he went to his great reward. We don't presume destination, just pass along the facts as they are: We say the poor son of a bitch died."

"I'd have fired you, Charley," Francis said, smiling as he poured another. There wasn't anyone there to drink it, but there would be. He kept them coming.

"You're a good man," I said. "Veritable saint."

Pearl joined us.

"Did the son of a bitch tell you it wasn't personal, Charley?" he said.

Arthur Pearl was my favorite photographer. He didn't think he was a fucking artist, like some photographers. He thought like a reporter. He worked like one, too, always digging, his camera a tool. Detail man. Clean lines, master of the telling expression. Some photographers could put their subjects at ease, but Pearl could disappear altogether. I don't guess I ever worked with a better one. But they sacked him, all the same.

"He did, Arthur. I was waiting for it, too. I said, 'If it wasn't personal, it would have been somebody else.'"

"It was, Charley," Pearl said. "Me."

⁕

I remember Madison, the metro columnist, walking in with an ex-wife on each arm, shouting, like always, "We have nothing to drink but beer itself," and then buying the house a round. It had been an old act for a long time, but it went down fine with that free beer. (Old newspaper adage: "We can't be bought, but we can be plied.")

Madison had been living off his reputation for years, but I didn't blame him so much. He'd become an institution, poor bastard. Or anyway, the newspaper version of an institution— drinks named for him in more than one dive bar, and his picture on a Memphis Area Transit Authority bus panel, a scowling mug with jowls and a devilish gleam in his eyes, and two words stamped out in black, in an old-style typewriter font, under the southernmost of his chins: "Get Mad."

Ah, Madison. I still liked him, because I was old enough. I could remember when he'd do anything for a column, go anywhere. He'd come in the newsroom some days with one eye socked black and a high stink rising. We'd cheer the man, and he hadn't even bought us a beer. We were drunk on the sight of him. He'd barge into the newsroom with some wild tale and bang it out. I've never seen a good writer write faster. He was a fierce thumper of the keys, but the words—God, they were something. Nobody ever captured this city better, a thousand words at a time. Madison did the ship-in-a-bottle trick some better. He put a whole fucking city in there, three times a week for twenty years.

He knew everybody and their next of kin. He knew the high and mighty, the men who ran Memphis, but he wasn't one of them, never would be, and so he worked them from the edges. He knew their mistresses and yard men. He knew where they got their hair cut and who cut it. He knew the pit masters of their favorite barbecue joints and whether they liked their pork shoulder pulled or chopped. For those powerful types dangerous enough to have henchmen, Madison knew the henchmen. Hell, he drank with them, chased women with them, and so the henchmen pulled their punches, but only a little, when they had to rough him up. It had to look real, after all, and anyway, it was good for his image to be a little beaten up. (Madison's eternal plea to the henchmen, or so he liked to say: "Do what you will to my face, boys. Just don't break any fingers, for I've a little typing to do later.") He had, in his prime, brought down a mayor, a bishop, two senators, an entire family of cotton barons, and councilmen enough to fill the Mid-South Coliseum to the cheap seats like it was the night of the Stax/Volt Yuletide Thing, 1968.

He loved the common man. They were his people. He was no better. His father was a lifelong factory worker who died on his feet, a heart attack, they said, at the last of his factory jobs, the headache powder plant out on President's Island. His mother cleaned houses for people who weren't even rich.

He'd ride shotgun with this old South Memphis rag-and-bone man on his daily rounds, Midtown and East Memphis, the better neighborhoods there, looking for whatever folks had put out on their curbs as trash—lawn mowers tossed the first time they wouldn't start and exercise bikes that had been ridden twice, and one time a litter of kittens. Abandoned kittens, Christ. It was like handing Madison the Pulitzer Prize on a platter with a slab of ribs and side of beans. He wrote that for a week and drank free for a month in every bar in Memphis. The whole town wept. I wept—and I'm a dog man. Those fucking kittens were more famous than the Peabody Ducks, there for a little while.

Lauderdale Slim—that was the name of the rag-and-bone man. He would appear once or twice a year in Madison's columns. Some said he didn't exist, that Madison made him up, concocted him, but that whorehouse lamp on his newsroom desk had to come from somewhere.

"Mad," I said. "I'm glad to see you, my man, but the circumstances like to kill me."

He stepped out of the arms of those ex-wives. He wobbled a bit and then seemed to steady himself. But he made the mistake of taking a step and began to pitch forward. One leg buckled and the other seemed to bend funny. I'd seen it happen one other time, in Hot Springs, Arkansas, to a horse. I froze, but those ex-wives swooped in and scooped him up. They seemed about to buckle, too, but were able, between the two of them, to bring him back up to standing. Muscle memory, I guess. If you married Madison, you were under no illusions about the heavy lifting being merely figurative. Or that the heavy lifting would end when the marriage did. But Madison seemed to have missed it all. (I think he'd missed entire marriages—he'd had six, counting the poor woman he married twice.) He stood and looked about the room, unruffled as ever, and said to me, "Who died, Charles?"

I didn't know whether he was that deep in denial, or that drunk, or whether it was both. But he seemed sincere in asking, and so I told the poor bastard.

"We did, Mad. We did."

*

I remember Tommy Miles, sitting alone at the bar. He was a copy editor, a desk rat, a somber little fellow at work, hunched over his keys and staring at the screen through round, wire glasses as if bewildered by the nonsense before him. He'd shake his head and set about to fix it. He could make sense of the worst rot. He was a savior of bad writers, could teach sentences to walk straight with proper bearing and go out into the world and say what they had to say, in plainspoken language. It was a gift, though the ink barons who owned us didn't value it so much, and less all the time. I don't even think the worst of the writers noticed—they didn't read a word of their rot, after they filed it. If they happened to notice, the next morning, that somehow it made sense, that it could speak plainly, if not quite sing, well, then … the newspaper sprites see to those things, don't they? Tommy Miles was a newspaper sprite. He was one in the flesh, bent-backed from his labor, with a smoker's teeth and a smoker's cough, looking ten years older than his age, but looking dapper, still and all, in that little tweed newsboy cap he always wore.

You'd see the slightest little smile start to form when he'd finish one story and move to the next. He'd pull back from the screen, never taking his eyes off it, and then lean back in and start again.

Some fall into their life's work and some are dragged, and most of both get by well and harmlessly enough. And some have no more business doing what they do than a rat does captaining a great ship (I've seen it happen countless times, though, with editors-in-chief). But a blessed few, by luck or grace or whatever name you give it, end up just where they should be, doing just what they should do. Jesus Christ our Lord and Savior had nothing on Thomas Patrick Miles, for that. He was a born copy editor, but now he was an ex-one.

He was hunched over a small glass of bourbon. I sat beside him.

"You poor bastard," I said.

"I never met one who wasn't," he said.

He leaned back then, as if from one of those stories. He turned and showed me that start of a smile, but then it died on his face—didn't stop or fade and start to turn to something else, but died. Then he stood and patted me on the shoulder, seeing the look of death upon me, too. He straightened that newsboy cap. Tipped it, just slightly. He turned and walked toward the door, in his head-down way, in those mincing steps of his. He walked like a very old sprite, though he wasn't yet fifty. He walked and kept walking and I never saw the poor bastard again.

✳

I remember punchlines to jokes, songs with curses for verses, and a dirty limerick about two sisters from Natchez, who forgot to batten their …

Filthy mouths and filthy minds, newspaper folk. They were my folk. I was theirs.

✳

And I remember sitting with Barboro and Stell at a table in back. He was our courts reporter and she was Queen of the Desk Rats. They were telling a young stranger about the business, the life, how dreadful a dodge it was—the low pay and long hours, all the hostility to our work, or worse, disregard—and how they would miss it so.

"We were our own country, our own small world," Stell said. "We each had our own tasks and tools. A civilization, is what I'm saying, even if not all of our lot were civilized. I loved everything about it. The language, most of all." She leaned back, took a healthy swig of beer. She smiled. Then she leaned into the young thing and said, "The words we used, you know, to describe what we did. We worked under threat of *deadlines*, and our library was called the *morgue*, and when a single word ended up alone on a line of type, like it had been abandoned by the rest of the sentence, left to fend, that was called a *widow*. When there was a story even Tommy Miles couldn't save, why, we *spiked* it—*killed* it. And I could tell you, too, what it means to *bleed*. I could show you the *gutter*."

Barboro said he loved the smell of ink. I did, too. It hit you, every day when you walked in the back door of the place. He said he dreamed some nights of drinking the stuff and other nights of swimming in it. He said he supposed he'd go to work in the family business now, the mortuary, but he didn't think he'd ever come to love the smell of embalming fluid. He didn't think he'd dream of drinking it or taking a dip. I wanted to ask what color it was, embalming fluid. (I didn't care. I just wanted to put words to work to describe it.) Was it like varnish or shellac or one of your clear liquors? Was it brown like bourbon, and could you sniff it like you would the good stuff, pick up woody notes of peat and regret? Did the smell of it hit you when you walked in the back door to work every day, lift you off the ground and rummage your senses, like ink did? Ah, ink. Goddamn, ink. That's how you send some poor soul out of this world, not with embalming fluid but ink, with an obituary, written proof of passage, letters of transit. (Old newspaper adage: Even God reads the obits.)

As they say, it's only twice most people get their names in the newspaper: when they're born and when they die. They're the lucky ones, I suppose. The ones we wrote about, mostly, had gotten up to no good, and lucky for us they had. Blank pages wouldn't do.

"I'd drink a shot of poison straight away," Stell said, raising her glass, "if I wasn't so attached to beer."

"You'll be all right, Stell," I said. "We all of us will."

"You don't believe that, Charley. You know better."

She turned again to our young stranger. She wagged a finger at him and then at me. "Now, this man here, this Charley Hull, he was one of the good ones. He was a reporter—a reputable thing to be, if you couldn't be a desk rat. He went out and found stories, Charley did. He pulled threads, overturned stones. He sorted through rubble. Sometimes it really was rubble—that hurricane down in New Orleans, and the tornado that blew some little Mississippi town clear across the state line to Alabama. Charley was a detail man. Forensic in his care. He'd find doll parts and love notes, the broken neck of a guitar, anything to make a story. Hell, one time a hank of gray hair! Damned if he didn't find the old woman it belonged to, some twenty miles away, in a school gym-turned-shelter, asking had anyone seen her cat named Peyton Manning."

It was a dog named Eli, but still.

"And he talked to people—Charley, who doesn't particularly care for people, as a lot. A loner, by nature. Professional introvert. No better at small talk, idle chat, than that ashtray there. And that—"

"You flatter me, Stell," I said. "I wish you'd go flatter some other poor son of a bitch."

"—is why he was so good at it, see. No better at human interaction than he was, why, he didn't pussyfoot around. Didn't know how. He'd ask what question needed to be asked. He'd blurt out what other reporters, ones with tact and social skills, would only slowly build up to—but they'd never quite get there. Couldn't bring themselves to ask it like it ought to be asked. Or would ask it, but just the once. But Charley Hull here—he'd not hedge or haw. Out with it! And he'd ask it as many times as need be. So here's to Charley Hull, one of the good ones! Charley Hull, who put his stunted social skills to work in the only way he could!"

Glasses were raised. Mine got as far as my lips.

"To Charley Hull," said Barboro. He made it sound like I really had died.

"And he had this other thing he'd do," Stell said. "It was classic Charley. He'd just stop talking. Wouldn't say another word—couldn't. It was such a chore, to gab on. So he'd just stop, mid-sentence. Some reporters—blowhards, basically, the business draws them in droves—talk all the time. They don't know what our man here was born knowing: You've got to shut up and listen."

The whole barroom seemed to go silent then. The whole world did. Or maybe I just like to remember it that way. How long? I don't know. An hour, a day, the length of a drink.

Stell finished her beer and caught Francis's attention for another, without as much as a raised eyebrow between them. Simpatico, those two. I sometimes wondered if they had the hots for each other. Do they still call them the hots? Anyway, the patron saint loved to pour those pints and the Queen of the Desk Rats loved to drink them down.

I took the opportunity to change the subject at the table, from yours truly to pretty much anything else. I looked up at the TV over the bar. "How about those Grizzlies?" I said. "They going to beat those fucking Clippers tonight?"

It was Game 6 of the NBA playoffs, Memphis needing a win to stay alive. Big doings of local import, though I wasn't much of a sports fan, really, and Stell said the game had gone to hell since the advent of baggy shorts.

"Nice try, Charley," she said to me, though she did offer a "fuck the Clippers," rather in the manner of a barroom motion.

"Fuck the Clippers!" came a chorus of chants.

Motion carried, drink to that, and then it was back to your man here, in all my stunted glory.

"But any fool can shut up," said Stell, back in the young stranger's face. "I heard of a sportswriter doing it once. But Charley, he was the master of the awkward pause, the stilted silence. Silence as an art. He'd just stop, with this look on his face

10

like desperation, like one more word and he'd die and take them with him. It's when they answered the question he'd asked seven times already. The awkward pause, the stilted silence—well, it's a form of torture, isn't it, Charley? People can't take it. They've got to *say* something. So they blather on. Masterful, how he did it. Even if it was only Charley being Charley, bringing his weaknesses to bear in the one job in life he was fit for."

The young stranger looked at me like I was lying in state, like I was his first dead body.

"It's OK, son. It's all pretty much true—the bad parts, anyway," I said. "I'm only about two dance steps above special, or whatever they call it these days. Like Stell here says, I found a career where I could put my lack of social skills to proper use. I brought my weaknesses to bear. It almost sounds profound, put that way."

"Christ—*profundity*," said Stell, who didn't touch the stuff.

# The stench of romance

Wick came. I knew he would. Wick, my best friend, raised his glass from across the barroom. He tilted it toward me, with a big, sad smile. I raised my glass and tilted it toward me, too, for I was fucked. I was fired, even if they wouldn't fucking call it what it was, and I didn't want to hear a word from God or the ghost of Horace Greeley or anybody who hadn't been sacked with the likes of me, but I could abide my best friend trying, as he would, to bring me up just a little. Good, old Wick. Wise head, Wick.

We found a quiet spot up front. The bar was a clothing store, ages ago, and we sat at a small table up in what used to be the window display area, like something for sale. Wick sat there like the latest fashion. I was last year's garb, marked down to move.

"Look at me, Wick," I said. "I'm a mess in gabardine."

I sat back and shrugged and scratched at the start of a tear in the left knee of my trousers. Yeah, I still call them trousers. I'm an old soul, I guess, or just a man out of time. So shoot me. Or pants me, whatever.

"That's not gabardine, Charley. That's just some mutt fabric, some cheap blend. You'll need to be dressing better, almost certainly, for whatever you do next." He looked me over, bit askance. "Even if it's vagrancy, or rock 'n' roll."

Wick dressed better, or at least he looked it. He was Old Money Memphis, and it showed. He had the way of the wealthy; he could wear anything, somebody's old rags or a find from the Bibles for China thrift store, and it would just drape from him like something bespoke. It's a wonder we ever met and became best friends, except that sort of thing could happen in Memphis, where a street of mansions was never more than a couple of blocks from a stretch of shacks.

We met playing sandlot football on a Saturday morning, in an empty lot midway between our homes. We bonded over our mutual disdain for the sport. I was only there tagging along with a buddy of mine, Winston, who was the star of the game. Wick was there because he'd heard some girls might be watching. We drifted from the game and started talking music, favorite bands. He loved R.E.M. and thought *Lifes Rich Pageant* was their best yet. He said the song "Fall on Me" was about the inherent meanness of the world. I said Springsteen's "Working on the Highway" was about the same thing, but Bruce said it straight out, didn't stoop to poetry, and gave it a better beat, and anyway if Springsteen had called an album *Lifes Rich Pageant,* which he wouldn't have, he wouldn't have forgotten the fucking apostrophe. Wick said I was pedantic and that it would hold me back in life and hurt me with girls. Twenty minutes together, and already we were talking like that. I wanted to punch him, or kiss him on the mouth, but we were spared from either, or both, because we soon found our common ground, our Memphis Saturday-morning sandlot, with Elvis Costello, whose latest, *King of America,* explained *everything* to us, or at least brought us to a higher plane of confusion.

When the game broke up, I said I knew about a party out in the country, out past Eads. He asked if there would be any girls there. I said I knew of one, at least. He said, "Will I have to fight you for her, Charley?" I said, "Nah, she's my cousin." He said, "Whatever you say, Jerry Lee."

Wick's grandfather founded Southern Life & Casualty, the insurance giant; the company headquarters was a twenty-two-story white-stone tower downtown on Court Square. The old man had it built special. Memphians of a certain age still called it "The Wick," because that's what they called the grandfather, and the building looked a little like one, long and skinny as it was. His father inherited the business and sold it. He founded an advertising agency down on old Cotton Row with a view of the river. The agency became the largest in the city and something of a regional concern. Wick inherited the agency and sold it; he founded a boutique firm he called a consultancy. His office was across the street from the bar, on the second floor of a renovated building that had been, for the longest time, a flophouse. He liked to joke that at the current rate of family decline, they were less than fifty years from future generations begging for cigs and candy on the hard streets of Memphis.

"I just wanted to say the word—gabardine," I said. I had this thing I liked to do, where I'd say words or phrases I'd never said before, places I'd never been or was like to go. Trichinosis, or Hey, Slick, or Cowbridge, west of Cardiff, in Wales. It kept the mind sharp and strangers at bay, or so I told myself. Wick would say it was why I never married, and I'd say I never married because I never found a woman who would have me, and Wick would say, "That's just what I got through saying, Charley."

We sat in silence for some time. It was my favorite thing about Wick, even more than the wisdom. He didn't have to talk every blessed second. I wondered if this was the secret of his consultancy's success, that he knew when to be wise and when to just be. So we sat and we drank. It was an Old Fashioned for him and I had a bourbon, neat, with my beer now. We sat there like serious old men with much to ponder. We might have been solving all the many woes of modern man, the dying industries and such, the fraught and fragile nature of life, of God's indifference. Human existence was a parlor trick. Life, a series of low blows. Love, a cruel mistress, or anyway, like God, indifferent. Still and all, I thought, I'm here, well lit, with my dear friend Wick, and proud of the way I made with my words, as long as they would let me. Much to be thankful for, it's true. But on the other hand, fuck-all. *Do I contradict myself? Very well then I contradict myself.* (I am drunk, I contain pints.)

"Just whatever you do, Wick, don't say I'm lucky."

"But you are, Charley."

"I guess you're going to say you envy me, too."

"I do."

The two of us sat at the small table, half looking out the window onto South Main, half back at the barroom full of poor bastards and sad wenches, talking and drinking and hugging, and dancing, a little, and crying, a little more.

"There's no other profession like it, Wick."

"There are other professions, though. Some of them—brace yourself, Charley—have better hours and better pay, bosses who are nearly human. Some of them don't even seem like jobs. You just might forget you're working."

"You talking about the Big Rock Candy Mountain, with that lake of stew and whiskey, too?"

"I'm just saying, Charley?"

"You think they have a newspaper there?"

"Where's that, Charley?"

"The Big Rock Candy Mountain. You think they have a newspaper? You think they have any openings for an experienced reporter? I'm willing to start at the bottom, cover night cops, or write obits. Hell, I'd write weddings. *The bride wore white lace and the groom a look of stunned bewilderment.*"

"C'mon, Charley. Forward march."

"Will work for stew. Whiskey, too."

"The future stands before you, Charley, all come hither."

"Ah, but the newspaper game, Wick. Nothing like it. Twenty-some-odd years and I think I covered everything but a duel—and we had one of those, near about, in the newsroom. Years ago, a reporter and assistant city editor. It was all over a comma, as I recall. I was just a wide-eyed cub, taking it all in. Imagine, Wick. A duel, or near about."

"It's why I prefer working alone."

"I'm just saying, Wick. There's no place like a newsroom."

"If you've seen one ghost town …"

"You know what I mean. How it used to be."

"I do, Charley. Good times. But gone. Not coming back."

I shrugged. I sighed. I took a sip. I tried to look to the future, but it was only the past that I saw. The past, poor and bedraggled, with a come-wither smile on its mug.

"So what the hell am I supposed to do now, Wick?"

"You can do anything you want, Charley. You decide."

"Nobody's going to pay me to drink bourbon."

"C'mon, Charley. You're a well-rounded man with interests. Why, you once—no, that was me."

I laughed, a little. It helped by a like amount.

"I'm a newspaperman, Wick. It's all the hell I've ever been or wanted to be. It's all I've ever given two damns about. Anyway, it's too late for me to wear socks that match."

I looked at my feet, at my socks that really were unmatched, and he stared out the window at some women walking by. He was happily married, to my cousin, but he took a sort of scholarly interest in women. He said he liked to keep a hand in, but it wasn't that. He liked to study them, the way some people do stamps or battlefield strategies,  or prints by Eggleston. It was the opposite of objectification. Wick marveled at women; he knew they were smarter than us and tougher than us, and already, secretly, ruled the world. He nodded at one now and said, "She walks like heaven's full up, and she's not one for crowds."

"What's that even mean, Wick?" But I knew. I saw her. Twenty-some-odd years of reporting and my powers of observation were finely honed. Ah, my powers. They seemed like carny barkings to me now.

"A woman like that," Wick said, "she's got other places she'd rather be. I envy her. You ought to, as well. Hoof it, Charley. Go forth and woo. She could be the one."

"You believe in that theory, do you?"

"I do."

"You would."

I scooted forward in my chair, as if I just might get up and give chase. But then I leaned back. She cantered on, out of view. I said she walked like she didn't want to be caught, at least by the likes of me. It had been a long time. It had been ages. Make of this information what you will, dear reader. I said, "Well," and then I did get up, but only to go take a piss.

I turned toward the back of the bar, took three steps, and about crashed into the barmaid. Molly O'Ghost, we called her. She was carrying a tray with beers, but still managed to catch me before I fell. She spun me back toward the pisser, all in full stride, without spilling a drop. It was like ballet, with thicker ankles.

Molly was an old woman, scowled all the time, and never had a kind word to say. We adored her.

I made my way without further incident. I stood in the pisser, looking at the wall in front of me. There were framed front pages of old papers proclaiming the vital news of crucial Memphis days. Machine Gun Kelly was captured, Boss Crump died, and the city elected its first Black mayor. There was an ice storm, and a wind storm that everybody called Hurricane Elvis. There were big headlines, and then, in small type that people mostly skipped over, the names of those who wrote the stories. I had stories on a couple of those pages. There was one from after the big storm, under the picture of an oak tree laid out across the roof of some poor son of a bitch's house, like a giant garnish. I remember standing in the front yard with him, talking about what terrible luck it was, for a tree to fall there, of all places, when we heard the shouts from across the street. They'd found a body inside, a little girl. (I'd tell you it was too sad for words, but there they were, framed and hanging over the pisser next to me, under my fucking name. But hell, if I hadn't written the story, somebody else would have.)

I finished and washed my hands, and looked at my mug in the mirror. The mug stared blankly back, like a dead man still trying to process the news of his demise, poor bastard.

Wick didn't miss me much.

"Look, here comes another, Charley. She walks like—"

"Emily know you're out drinking, watching women go by?"

Emily was Wick's wife and my cousin. She was a poet. Hell, she was a poem—one of those epics about death and grace and the great river, disappearing around the curve of its bends on a summer morn, with mist, and yellow warblers singing. Christ, can't you hear them sing? She could speak four languages, cuss like a stevedore, drink like the Gashouse Gang, and shoot a gun like Stagger Lee. (While Wick studied women, I studied Emily. I think that may well be the opposite of the opposite of objectification.) I don't know how a cousin of mine came across such an array of talents. I asked her one time, and she said she won them in a card game with nothing but a pair of nines and a gin smirk. Seemed plausible.

"You've got the best wife," I said.

"Get your own," Wick said.

(I'd just about married once. Short story. Tell you later.)

"They keep getting away," I said, "while here I sit. Look at 'em go."

I fell into Wick's field of study. I called on my finely honed powers of observation. Maybe later I'd move on to card tricks that surprised even me, or I'd levitate an ashtray to the astonishment of all. I'd make the jukebox play backward and watch the dancers all fall down and out of love. I'd win bar bets and give performances that drew standing-room crowds, take the show on the road to critical acclaim, play theaters, and the summer shed circuit. I'd open for Dylan, and he'd call me onstage to sing with him, "It Takes a Lot to Laugh, It Takes a Train to Cry," or something from the *Desire* album, my favorite of his. Ah, the future was boundless. If only it would take its foot off my windpipe and stop mocking my powers.

I stared out the window. Memphis did not seem to be observing my misery. It went on like nothing had happened. There was a woman, early twenties, her hair blue-tipped and buds in her ears, listening to some song, her walk the nearest thing to a waltz. There were two more, all bare legs, in tanned lockstep, laughing at some fool thing a man had done, no doubt. There was another in gabardine, I swear, and I just about took off after her. I'd tell her my sad news and ask if she wanted to go away, to start life anew. She'd ask where, and I'd say, "Cowbridge, west of Cardiff, in Wales."

Or maybe I imagined this last one. I don't know. Then a man walked by. He walked like a caveman on a Monday, like he was on his way to club something and call it supper. The men mostly all walked that way. There was no mystery to the beasts. I thought of my own father, the son of a bitch, but Wick saved me, good man.

"What's on your mind, Charley?" Wick said. "You have that look you sometimes get."

"Nothing. Just stuff and things. Why I never married, what I'll do next, regrets, dying industries, just exactly what God's been up to all this time. You know, life's rich pageant and all."

(We still argued about R.E.M. and agreed on Elvis Costello.)

"Anyway," he said, "it was Emily who sent me."

"She worried about me?"

"We're both worried about you."

"I thought I was lucky. I thought you envied me."

Wick leaned back and smiled and said, "Be that as it may." That's what Wick said when somebody had him cornered in conversation. But Wick never got cornered, not really, except on purpose. Wick had levels. Wick had cellars and attics, trapdoors and cubby holes, drawers with false bottoms. He understood people. He knew that sometimes the other person needed to win, even if it was a small victory that wouldn't survive the crushing blows of larger warfare. He knew when to jab, too; he knew that sometimes one man's jabs were all that kept the other man upright and standing. (It's how he was playing me now.) Wick was three moves, six weeks, and several maudlin dramas ahead of the rest of us. (He was ahead of everybody but Emily.)

"Ah, fuck me, Wick."

"That's it, Charley, get them out. All those words you could never say in the paper."

"Fuck, piss, chimera."

"You couldn't say chimera in the newspaper?"

"You know how they made us write on a sixth-grade level."

"You know what it means?"

"Chimera?"

"Yeah."

"No."

"Well, maybe that's why they wouldn't let you say it."

"Fuck you."

We laughed.

Wick had talked wiser men than me out of suicide, duels, divorce, drinking pure grain, and playing too much classic country on the jukebox. Classic country, he said, was good in small doses but in larger ones brought on suicide, duels, divorce, drinking pure grain, and more classic country on the jukebox. He said it was an endless spiral of something, I forget what. He said it was a scientific principle with a name, but I forget that, too. For those low moments we all face, Wick prescribed something by Bobby "Blue" Bland, "Two Steps from the Blues" or "Cry Cry Cry." He said Bobby "Blue" sang the saddest songs ever, but wore sharkskin suits and made all the women moan.

Wick got a lot of this from his father, a wise and sweet man who walked like—well, he was just slightly effeminate, if you want to know the truth. He walked like life had just told him the secret to bird flight. He was as much like my father as a wing was a fist.

"Fucking fuck me, fucker," I said. "I'm fucked. We're all of us fucked."

I crossed my legs and scratched some more at that start of a tear in my trousers.

"Well, not you," I said. "You're fine. I speak, rather, of us fucked ex-newspaper folk."

"Ah, the former ink-stained wretches, set free to be something new." He looked out across the barroom. "Well, they all look to be coping about as well as you, Charley."

I told him about Barboro and the mortuary. "Will says it'll be like dying twice in a week. But he may have no choice, with his older boy in college at Rhodes and two more coming up." I told him Stell was just working because she loved it, but the Lord God in green eyeshade, how she loved it. She was almost as rich as Wick. She had family money and then married more, though she didn't marry well. She married a cad—if they still call them that. He did white-collar time, but it didn't change him, and he still had most of his money. He and Stell were still married but living apart. No matter. She was hitched to the newspaper, like so many of us. "She said she figures she'll travel, get away," I said.

"I asked her where, and she just said, 'Hell, I don't know.' She said it like Hell was some place you could take the train to, like Chicago." And I told him about Flippen. "He'll go into politics, after covering city hall. You watch. He'll be a flack or fixer. He'll be running this city inside a year, and indicted in five. I don't think he'll be able to help himself, set free on a corrupt city with no need for his newspaper ethics. He knows every devious trick's ever been done. Good man."

"You think this city's corrupt?"

"They're all corrupt, Wick. It's why there are newspapers."

"Did Bogie say that in 'Deadline—U.S.A.'?"

"You're just sore because Bogie never played a consultant in a movie. Bogie ate consultants for breakfast."

"I don't think there were consultants in Bogie's day."

"Because he ate them all," I said, "for breakfast."

I took a sip of bourbon and then of beer. I told him about a few more of our sorry lot. I said Vollintine, the sacked city editor, might want to go into the preaching game, after that benediction he gave. I said Mad would probably live on his legend, and the charity of all those ex-wives. I said, "Ah, well. We'll be OK, most of us, in time. But I'm worried for James Ricketts. He's young, you know. I seriously think he'll do something romantic like jump off one of the railroad bridges, the Frisco or the Harahan. He's got his whole life ahead, but he's a born newspaperman, born too late. Kid's got talent for the trade but no place to ply it. He could go to some other town, some other paper, but hell, it's the same everywhere. He'd be chasing his own ass."

"Poor Jimmy Ricketts—sounds like some Dickensian waif," Wick said.

"Might as well be," I said. "At least most of us got a good run of the business. We knew it when newspapers were kings and made more money than God and Southern Life & Casualty combined, even if the owners didn't share it much. We knew it when it had the stench of romance, when what we did mattered. People read us over coffee mugs in the morning and cursed us or said, 'Damn straight,' or 'Did you see what the son of a bitch said today?' and—"

"Ah, the stench of romance," Wick said.

"Can you smell it, Wick?"

"No, only you all ever could. It's an odorless gas to the rest of us. But apparently not a lethal one."

"You think it's just been us smelling our own bullshit, all along?"

"I do," he said, not unkindly. "You newspaper types always were snobs. You know that, don't you? Like everybody else in the world was playing with pretty dolls and toy trains and pick-up sticks, and that game where you try to conquer the world with dice and little, tiny soldiers. Nobody was anything to you all, really—not the politicians or the magnates or God forbid the common man. You all owned the common man—he was yours. You kept him in your pocket with your pens and change, book of matches from The Lamplighter. Nobody mattered. Not really. Because you all had—"

"The hell are you talking about Wick?" But I knew.

"—the truth. Ah, you all and the truth. Like the truth was some unstable element or mummified pharaoh, and only you all were fit to handle it. The truth. Ha! You'd parade it out like it was a real thing. The most cynical lot of people on this great rock, you newspaper types—don't believe in God, or that Babe Ruth called his shot, don't believe in anything except the truth. But your truth, Charley, the newspaper truth, was never quite the *true* truth, was it? How many times did I hear you say it—that you couldn't write but a fraction of what you knew? That what you did write was half the truth, or less. Was a fraction. And a fraction of the truth is a fraction of a lie. That's what you'd say."

"I said a lot of things when I was drinking, Wick."

"Yeah, and that's when I found out what was really going on in this town—the story you knew but couldn't write." He raised his glass and tipped it. "Alcohol is better for getting the truth than ink, my friend."

"Somebody old and wise and dead say that?"

"My father may have. Sounds like something he'd say."

"I miss your father."

"You had your own. I don't guess you miss him."

I didn't say anything to that. I said, "So we've been fooling you, the reading public, all these years, or trying to."

"No, Charley, no. Fooling yourselves. Though I suppose the ink barons knew it was just a product they were peddling. And you were just their workers, making their product. Building it from what materials you had at hand. You were a tradesman, working a trade. Not a bad thing to be, sure. But a trade—that's all the hell it ever was. For the longest time, you didn't need to go to college to learn to do it. I still don't see how that ever changed. I don't see how they tricked you into going to college for it and still paid you like tradesmen. But who was to blame for that? It was you all, bragging about jobs with long hours and low pay, and those ink barons, they sat back and smiled every time."

"Tradesmen," I said.

"Sure. You were apprentices and novices and so forth, and then you learned it—your trade. Good for you! You dipped your beaks in barrels of ink, like that dippy bird toy Old Man What's-His-Name invented."

"He didn't invent the dippy bird thing. He bought the patent for it from some poor bastard for a few hundred dollars, and then sold millions of the things. Fucking dippy birds."

"That's your problem. You have no respect for visionaries—and a hometown one, no less. A man who had the foresight to see the financial boon in fucking dippy birds, as you call them—think of it. That's some kind of brilliance, if you ask me. You despise vision and hate on the visionary. All your admiration and sympathy goes to the poor bastards. It's like they're your pets. You walk them around on a leash, like you own them."

"I don't know what you're talking about."

"You know exactly what I'm talking about, Charley. I'm talking about you newspaper types. How you came to be and why. It was all very noble, of course. I'll give you that. You wrote stories and gave them headlines big as tombstones and brought down some crooks, it's true. But are there less crooks in the world because of it?"

"Fewer, not less."

"You're still pedantic."

"Fuck the Clippers," I said, "and fuck you, too."

We laughed. We leaned in and hugged. We settled back and let the wake swell about us.

Flippen was standing on a chair, arms aloft, as if gesturing to God, but probably only to Barboro, who wasn't listening, too busy hitting on a bottle of wine. Stell had the young stranger by the chin, delicately almost, as if deciding whether he was ready to hear the hard truth about life. And Pearl, he was slow dancing alone at the jukebox to an old Stax ballad by the Soul Children, "I'll Be the Other Woman," his white shirt untucked and seeming to hover about him, like smoke showing off.

When I turned back, Wick was standing to go. I stood, too.

"I'll walk you out."

"No need, Charley. It's just a bar. I don't know my way out quite as well as I know my way in, but I'll find it."

"I could use a bit of air, anyway."

"Sure, then."

# Dixie-fried Narnia

We stood out on the sidewalk. We didn't say anything. I supposed Wick would go home to Emily. I'd go back to the wake, and … what? I didn't know. I didn't want to go home. There was nothing and nobody for me there. I didn't even have a fucking dog. Maybe I'd get drunk enough to go and piss on the front lawn of the editor-in-chief. It was as grand a gesture as I could conjure in the moment. He lived in Chickasaw Gardens, a big, fine, stately manse. He'd hear me rustling in the shrubs, watering the things. He'd wake up and wonder what the hell. He'd plead with me to leave and I'd go on pissing. Maybe I'd sing that song by the Pogues about going where streams of whiskey were flowing. I'd probably get arrested and thrown in the can—like Wales, a place I'd never been.

Wick looked at me and seemed to catch a gleam of a dangerous sort.

"Walk with me, Charley," he said. "I want you to see something."

He started off. I turned and looked back inside the window of the bar, as if I might see myself, still up there drinking in the display area, like some kind of mannequin gone to seed.

"C'mon, Charley."

I fell in with him. I asked where we were going.

"Just down here a little ways," he said.

We walked past an art gallery, a coffee shop, and a new restaurant with a name I couldn't pronounce. I didn't think it was a real word. I asked Wick if he and Emily had eaten there. I knew they would have. They were social people and adventurous eaters. They probably knew the chef. I didn't know how Memphis had become a town where chefs were as renowned as basketball players and soul singers. Sure enough, Wick said he had the duck confit grilled cheese and Emily had something with arugula. I asked if, on the whole, he'd rather have been at Payne's eating a barbecue sandwich. Payne's was over on Lamar, in an old, converted gas station. But it was about the best barbecue joint in a town busting with them.

"Of course," he said, "but it was one of those business dinners, you know. New client, just started doing some work here. A developer. He's doing something with the old Tuck Building. He doesn't know what—just something. He'd read about this new restaurant in *The New York Times* or somewhere." It's true, the Gray Lady was sniffing around the kitchens of Memphis. "He just had to go there. So we did. It was good. That's all, Charley."

"Do you even know what confit means, Wick?"

"I think it just means cooked in its own fat, Charley."

"What they ought to do with the chef."

"You know, it's all right for us to have some fancy restaurants with colorful food and funny names. It's still Memphis, in the end. We're not about to become Paris or Brussels or God forbid Nashville, Athens of the South."

I said I hoped to hell he was right. My idea of fine dining was sitting at the counter of some barbecue joint eating a pork shoulder sandwich so big and messy they had to hose you down after. Give me a side of beans and a bag of chips and a cold one to drink. The chips, if they were the local brand, would have a Bible verse on them. *In his town there were many joints, and they all served barbecue.* Well, it used to be that way. It was changing, I feared. The world was—I knew that. But Memphis? Did it have to change, too? Who could I see about this? Whose lawn did I have to piss on?

"Never change, Memphis," I said to my city on the bluff. "Stay true to me, ol' gal."

"What that's, Charley?"

"Nothing, Wick."

"Well, catch up, man. It's right here."

We stood in front of an abandoned storefront. I'd noticed it before—one of those strange Memphis sights. There was nothing behind the storefront. The building itself had been razed while three-story buildings still stood on each side of it. Only a facade remained here. They'd put plywood panels over where the windows had been, and on the panels someone painted a sort of Great Plains scene of big sky and vast flat land and a small herd of buffalo. There was a girl in a dress in the scene, too, but it was impossible to know if she was fleeing or frolicking or what. She seemed somewhat of a ghost girl. She hovered just above the ground and tilted slightly. She had skinny legs and knobby little knees, and a dazed kind of look on her plain face. She just had a down-sloping line for a mouth. I leaned forward to study the scene, then leaned back and shrugged. Wick shrugged, too. Memphis being a place where, sometimes, things don't mean anything. They just are.

Wick was at the door now. It was padlocked, but he had the key.

"What in hell, Wick?"

"Look here, Charley."

He swung open the door and stepped back. There were trees and vines, weeds and wild flowers. It was a goddamned forest in there. It was dark as a jungle. I half-expected some rangy beast or feral being to come swinging from the darkness, yelling something all wild and twangy.

"Jesus, Wick. It's like some Dixie-fried Narnia in there," I said.

"It's mine, Charley. I bought the son of a bitch."

"What exactly did you buy?" There was nothing there, and yet there was a world in there. I took half a step toward the door, but Wick stopped me.

"Careful. When they tore the building down, they went deep. No telling what's down there."

"You bought this?"

"I did."

"Without setting foot inside?"

"Yes."

"Why, exactly?"

"It's the damnedest thing—I don't know. I got the idea after having dinner with that client from out of town, the one who bought the Tuck Building. But it's different, you know. He doesn't know what he'll do with his building, but he'll damned sure do something. Lofts, probably. He spent money on it, so he'll expect money back. He's a businessman. Me? I'm just descended from businessmen. So I can just—"

"You're not going to do anything with it, are you, Wick? You're going to keep it like it is."

"That's my current line of thinking, yeah. Until something better comes along. We'll see."

"Until something better comes along—I think you just gave me a title for my memoir."

"You writing your memoir, Charley?"

"Fuck, no. Just saying."

"Well."

We stood peering in. We stepped back. It changed, depending on the distance and angle. It became foreign lands and other worlds and the realm of storybooks. From across the street, with the door thrown open, it looked like the deepest woods. A bear might have ambled out.

We sat on the curb, looking at it for the longest time.

"I thought the same thing, you know—Narnia," Wick said. "My mother, she read me all those books when I was a kid."

Wick had that look he got when he talked about his folks. I had that look I got when somebody who had normal, decent, caring parents talked about them. My father beat my mother blue. He'd give her the back of his hand and then stand over her like some referee might come up and raise his hand in victory. My father was a brute. He worked forty years for Memphis Light, Gas and Water, never missed a day, and then retired. He lived another ten in brutish leisure. He died peacefully, in his sleep, in his easy chair, with a war movie on. It was an old favorite of his. The screen was filled with smoke and rubble and that whole blood-waltz-of-war thing some men love. He'd never have called it that, of course. My father didn't trust words, and used them mostly as a recourse, when grunts and glares failed him. They seldom did.

28

He died with the movie credits playing, a near-empty can of Schlitz on the table beside him, and a cigar stub in the ashtray. If ever a man deserved to be electrocuted on the job, it was my father. Some nights, I prayed it would happen, for my mother's sake, for both our sakes. But God did everything but tuck the son of a bitch in for the night. He managed even to take it with him when he went—or anyway, he left nothing much behind but the dregs of that beer, that cigar stub, debts to his bookie, and my mother's blue heart. He beat that, too. It was his favorite target. Or maybe it was her favorite place to be hit. They were complicated, those two.

"We didn't have books in my house, so much," I said. "We got the newspaper so my father could see if his teams won—the teams he'd bet on. Or the dogs, horses, whatever. My father would bet on whether it would rain buckets on Wednesday afternoon. So I picked up the newspaper because it was around. It was something I could hold up and hide behind. That's how it began, with me and newspapers. I guess I've been hiding behind them ever since—that what you've been getting at, Wick?"

I wanted him to jab me again, just to keep me upright and standing. Or maybe I wanted a punch in the mug, to snap me out of whatever I might sink into, the mess I was and the worse mess I would become, until something better came along.

But Wick said, "Your father—if he was around now, they'd explain him away with names and treat him with pills."

"Maybe he was just a son of a bitch."

"You're always looking for the simple explanation to everything, Charley. It's the newspaperman in you, I guess. But life's not really like that. You know that, don't you?"

"We had to keep it simple, Wick. We had to put one out every day."

"I know. I'm just saying—your father. I don't know. Hell, Charley."

"He was a bastard, Wick."

"Maybe he had some sort of imbalance."

"Like he was more beast than man?" I looked again to see if that bear might amble out.

"I'm trying to help, Charley. I am. I don't want you to think you're damaged goods, just because your folks had, I don't know, issues."

"I know, Wick. You're a good man, a good friend. You come from good stock—that counts. It matters. It's the reason you're sitting here now, trying to help. I appreciate the hell out of it. I do."

On those nights when I'd pray my father would be electrocuted on a city light pole, fried on a stick like some treat at the Mid-South Fair, I imagined Wick's family would take me in, and Wick would be my brother, and Wick's father would be my father. (In this scenario, would Emily no longer be my cousin? Would we no more be kin?)

I never could quite reconcile what would happen with our mothers, in this scenario. They were as different as they could be, too. Wick's was quiet but sly. She was a professor of literature at Rhodes and preferred the company of her favorite characters. Her hair was usually mussed, and she'd go about in this baggy old sweater that was a shade of gray Wick and his father loved to try to guess. Battleship? Confederate Army? Russian winter? She'd look up from some book and smile that sly smile of hers. Then she'd go back to reading and they'd let her be. I don't know how much outright passion there was in the marriage, but there was a deep appreciation. At any rate, theirs was a quiet house. Quiet can be nice, or so I hear. Our house was loud. My mother's brooding could drown out my father's beloved war movies. She'd poke and provoke, and he'd do what any old bear would do. They were a Tennessee Williams play that went twelve rounds instead of three acts. Maybe I'd write a book about them. I'd write that memoir, in lieu of honest work or a good idea. Ah, see the future opening up for me now, with fangs, and a breath to fell entire armies.

"My mother couldn't sit still long enough to read the warnings on her pill bottles," I said.

"You're nothing like them, Charley. You aren't. It's more like you're a reaction against them. Like some kind of recoil—like you saw them, how they were, the mess they made of things, and decided at a young age that you'd just sort of live outside of it all. You wouldn't throw yourself into life, for fear you'd become your father or your mother, or God forbid some combination."

"I'd have been a touchdown favorite over the Tokyo skyline, if that had happened." I feigned a pose that was part Godzilla, part Heisman Trophy.

We laughed. We hugged again. Then he was off for home. I went back to the wake, near as I can remember …

# Tough birds and bitter angels

Molly O'Ghost greeted me with a fresh pint. I remember that.

"Did you know the newspaper's dying, Molly?" I said.

"I'd heard it was doing poorly," she said, with the exact measure of sympathy you'd expect from a woman who'd buried three husbands and spent her days serving drinks to drunks.

She was a tough bird, but we didn't mind the guff she gave us. We didn't come to the bar to have our cheeks brushed or be called dear. We didn't come to escape life but to look it deeper in its one good eye. We came to drink and cuss our editors and the corporate overlords who owned us. We came to rail against the fates, and revel in the long hours and low pay, and to make like money was nothing to us, like we had a higher purpose. Wick was right. We really thought everybody else was playing with dolls and toy trains, and that game with the dice and little, tiny soldiers. We were doing the important work. We were the chroniclers of crucial days.

We thought even our drinking had a higher purpose. It was church to us, this place. It was more: The bar was an extension of the newsroom. It was our locker room, our clubhouse, our secret bunker hideout. We could be the worst of ourselves there. We could let our bitter natures roam free. Ah, our bitter natures. Our better angels, too—they came to the bar, as well, to be corrupted by, made bitter by, the likes of us. That's how we thought. We did. We thought that's what made us charming, all of it, but secretly I think we knew better. Sometimes we'd even vow to change. I told Molly one time I was going to stop being an asshole. She said, "They got a patch for that, Charley? Gum?"

*

Then Arthur Pearl, my favorite photographer, was holding court. He was as good at spinning wild tales as he was slow-dancing alone or capturing small moments in camera snaps. Then he could turn around and go full monk (or Monk, to a T), not speak for hours except to say the most telling little thing you ever heard, if only you understood. One time we rode together, on assignment, to the Gulf Coast after Katrina. He drove, so the car stereo was under his control—rules of the road. We spent the whole way down listening to jazz—*Monk's Dream*, the album with "Bright Mississippi," trying to bring us up, buoy us against what was coming, and then, seeming to say *fuck it, bring it on*, he switched to *Black Beauty* by Miles, live at Fillmore West, a sort of moody storm set to music. Just outside of Ocean Springs, we came upon a small house with a kitchen table and chairs strewn about the yard. The front porch was bitten off by some beast— looked bitten off—and the roof punched out—seemed punched out—and Pearl said, "We'll stop here. Somewhere inside, there'll be some untouched little something. There tends to be, after a hurricane." We stopped and got out. Just then, the owner came from around the side, a ball-capped guy about our age, looking hangdog and half-dazed, with a couch cushion under one arm. The other arm hung half-limp from its socket. He half-waved to us. We told him who we were and he fell right into his story, like people do. He invited us in, showed us his son's room, took us straight there, all the windows and a wall missing, the floor a jigsaw puzzle of broken glass—and there it was, as foretold by Pearl, the son's perfectly made bed, untouched. The man said his son had been away, at his grandparents' in Birmingham, and when he came home and saw his bed unmussed, it might make the rest of it seem a little less scary. He said his wife died, two years before. Cancer, he said. I didn't ask what kind but I found out, later, just by asking about other things. I felt like a sneak, but that's the job. Anyway, now it was just the two of them, a dad and his eight-year-old son.

Then the man just stood staring as we went to work, taking in the scene with our particular tools, Pearl with his camera and me with a pen and notebook. Tools for telling a story. A story: Sometimes it seemed like a small, meaningless thing, but never when you were in the midst of it. Then it seemed almost spiritual. Or was that just what we told ourselves?

We thanked him for sharing his troubles and letting us intrude. He thanked us for caring. We just nodded. What were we supposed to say to that? We did. Care, I mean. But that's not why we were there.

He walked us to the car and then turned back to look at what was left of his house. I wished him luck, and he shrugged and said, "God's good." I didn't say either way. I just turned to Pearl, who nodded again. He didn't say anything the whole way home, either. He didn't even play any jazz on the car stereo. Maybe it's like Miles said. Jazz isn't about the notes you play but the notes you don't.

But now, at the bar, Pearl had a crowd around him. He was a showman, a master at play. Hell, I guess he was an artist, after all. He was Miles at the Fillmore, Bird at Birdland …

"Blood and floods and that one time lightning struck a preacher in the middle of a baptism," he said. "Swear to God. Hatchie River, out near Bolivar. I was there to shoot the baptism for a Sunday spread. The lightning was on account of God loved me more than He did that preacher. But the preacher lived to tell, and tell it he did. Said he was touched by the Almighty. Said he was chosen. Looked like to me God was going gigging for preachers down by the river that day and found Him a fat one. Lit him up like Beale Street neon in the rain. We saw bones and innards, brains and gold fillings, down on the banks of the Hatchie that day."

We all laughed, but he was already onto the next story.

"Blues kings in Cadillacs with corncob pipes. An old soul man with his cane—it had the Stax Records finger-snapping logo, in gold, for a head. And that one day with the original crazy white boy, Jerry Lee Lewis, down at his ranch in Nesbit, just south of town. He drank whiskey from a silver goblet and told us some of the crazy shit he'd done, setting pianos aflame and shooting guns at ghosts, and one time, in Beaumont I think it was, a girl climbed up on the stage, middle of 'Breathless,' spring of nineteen and fifty-eight, and collapsed at his feet. He said girls were always collapsing at his feet in those days. Usually, he said, they'd get back up and start climbing him. But this one was dead as Beaumont on a Tuesday. Killer claimed he brought her back with the laying on of a single hand. Said the right hand saved the girl and the left kept the beat. 'Gospel truth,' he said. I just kept shooting as he talked. The sight of him: his mouth elastic, like all the best singers. A mouth like cartoon rubber. Torch-lit eyes. One leg twitching like he might have felt some young thing, beginning her fresh ascent. Then he raised that right hand, gazed at the thing. Reporter on the story, local girl, white girl, not two years out of J-school, she like to died, herself."

Somebody recalled the girl's name. Cilla Pine.

"She told me on the drive back up to Memphis that she'd seen priests look at chalices that way," Pearl said. "I told her to put it in the story, but she didn't."

Somebody, it might have been me, said, "I don't guess J-school prepared her for the one and only Jerry Lee Lewis, but I'm sure St. Agnes Academy did its best."

"She's at *The New York Times* now," Stell said. "I see her stories sometimes. She's pretty damned good. But what about it, Arthur? You think she's still leaving out the best bits?"

But he was off again. It was tornadoes now.

"The things you'd see, after. Houses down to splinters and trees to twigs, and one time—true story, mostly—an oil painting of the thirty-ninth and forty-third governor of Mississippi, Theodore G. Bilbo, the racist little fuck himself, impaled in the left eye by a fireplace poker, in what was left of the drawing room of an antebellum mansion in Holly Springs."

Another drink, and then: "Tornadoes don't always hit trailer parks, you know. But mostly they do. One time I saw three stacked like a child's blocks. Earle, Arkansas. Man in the top trailer claimed to have slept through it all. Stuck his mug out a window and grinned real big at me. Said God was good but white lightning was better."

Now he leaned forward, and in a confessional tone said, "Give me a tornado and you can have the rapture. Because with a tornado, there's work to do after. People to search for. Possessions to sort through. Photographs to take, to mark the day, to make it whole, remind people what happened and who suffered. I'm not saying I do—*did*—life-saving work with my camera. I'm not."

"Life-affirming." I don't remember who said it.

Pearl thought about that. "Hell," he said. "That's more than God can say, some days."

We all laughed, and Pearl said, "Good times. Even the bad ones. Some of the bad ones were the best of all. Don't know what in hell I'll do now. Guess I'll just go and shoot myself, huh?"

A barroom version of a chorus of hallelujahs now. A slurry of amens.

He raised his hands like he was holding a camera, then made a clicking motion, but instead of a click sound, he made a *pow*.

✳

Then it was Vollintine, telling wonderfully filthy stories—so much for his budding career as a preacher. He'd been a good city editor, as city editors go, and now he was a sacked one. Stell was there, and Barboro. Flippen. Pearl had gone, presumably not to shoot himself. There was a young reporter called Kitty something, I never could remember. I didn't know what happened to Madison. Young James Ricketts never did show.

I caught the end of Vollintine's story—*and the drunken sot of a sitting judge he said to the woman, 'Why, you twat of the walk!'*—and there was laughter all around, and then another round.

"Ah, Charley Hull," said Vollintine, greeting me. "What will you do, now that you've been shucked?"

"Hell, I don't know, Vol. I can't even fathom it." I shrugged. "My friend Wick says I can be anything I want. My friend Wick, he says we're lucky, all of us. Said he envies us."

"Do you feel lucky, Charley?" Stell said.

36

"I feel like a bus hit me, and my good friend keeps telling me to cheer up—it could have been a train."

"It was a train hit me," Barboro said. The drink seemed to have taken him all of the sudden, like the drink will. He would be calling out train stops in a few minutes.

Kitty Something, barely with us a year and sacked like the rest of us, had a look of concern. But Flippen said, "Don't mind Barboro. A train hit him and knocked him into the drink. He'll be alright."

"Like hell I will," said Barboro. He had the look that pacifists get when they need to punch something, but don't know the first thing about it. Stell patted his cheek with her cigarette hand, to calm him; it was a small, tender moment and I watched the good reporters at the table watch it—the slow swipe of the cigarette and the nearness of fire to skin, the ashes left behind on his collar, scattered there, and the smoke like an aura around her hand— with the fascination and attention to detail that the best reporters watch *everything*.

Barboro drew calm. He tried for a smile, but settled for a drink. Good man.

*

And there was Blessin' Larry, a neighborhood figure of renown, if by renown you mean purveyor of pills and pilfered goods and sometimes surprisingly accurate political gossip. He worked the side streets and alleys on the south end of downtown. A tall, skinny bent thing of a man, smelled like a garbage scow in July, but essentially harmless—once sold me an alleged lock of Sputnik Monroe's hair. I didn't want it, exactly, but Blessin' was a canny salesman. He'd position himself just upwind of you, with a wall at your back, and then gab and spiel you until you agreed to some purchase. It was like a toll you paid to get past him. Then he would bless you, hence the name. Larry may or may not have been his actual first name and his surname was a mystery to all, though I once heard he was descended from one of the founders of Memphis—Winchester, Jackson, or Overton, I wasn't sure which. Jackson, I'm guessing.

He'd been thrown out of so many businesses he didn't bother anymore, but he'd slipped inside Little Blind's and was working the crowd. He must have been disappointed to learn we no longer had need or use for political gossip and were beyond blessin', but maybe he'd find some takers for his pills. I wondered did he have any that turned back time ...

*

And I remember running into the young stranger at the jukebox. He was studying the thing like a budding artist would the old masters. I noticed a guitar case at his feet. He wore jeans and a red T-shirt, and what I made out to be a thrift-store sport coat. I wondered if it was from the Bibles for China spring collection. But I doubted it. He seemed new to town. There seemed about him an air of innocence that Memphis had not yet taken out of him. He had a bird's nest of brown curls that matched his sport coat.

"So you're a musician," I said.

"We were supposed to play here tonight. Well, we asked if we could play, and the owner—I think he was the owner, acted like he owned the place—said to go ahead and play if we wanted. He said it wouldn't get crowded until late, and so we couldn't do much damage with nobody here, and by the time it got crowded nobody would be able to hear us, anyway. He said we could put a bucket out, but not to be surprised if some drunk thinks it's to piss in. He didn't say there was going to be a wake."

"Where's the rest of your band?"

"Well, it's just me and my girlfriend. But she—"

He shrugged and dropped his head.

"She run off on you?"

He couldn't bring himself to say it, so I said, "Ah, she'll be back." I didn't believe it, of course. She'd be halfway to the Gulf

Coast, with a long, pale leg out the passenger-side window of some bad man's roadster, showing Mississippi her new tattoo.

"You think?" I could see it in his eyes. He didn't believe it either. But then he smiled, as if another thought entirely had struck him. It had. "I'm socially stunted, too, aren't I? Like Stell said about you, Charley. I think I just realized it." He dropped his head again, and then brought it up, blushing. "Always thought I was just sensitive, you know. Introspective."

"And yet you get up in front of people and sing?" I said.

"Oh, no. I don't sing. Hardly at all. I write the songs and play guitar. It's my girlfriend who sings. She's the reason we even have a band—well, call ourselves a band. We call ourselves the Church Keys, on account of the dichotomy of it. A church key, to open a can of beer with. Anyway, I'm the quiet one—quiet as church, she says. I stand back and off to the side. I don't like cliffs, so much, you know. That's what the stage is to me—a cliff. But my girlfriend—well, call her my girlfriend—she's out there on the edge with her eyes closed, singing some old murder ballad like it was her who did the killing. She's got this spooky little croon. I just stand back and try to remember to keep strumming. I guess without her, I'll just—"

"Don't worry," I said. "You'll go it alone. You in all your stunted glory."

"I thought you said she'd come back."

He sort of smiled, and I did, too.

"Anyway," I said. "Use what you've got. Stay quiet. It's fine to be quiet. You see more, when you listen. Use your heartbreak, too. It's tough, sure, but good God, the songs you'll get out of it."

"You think?" he said again. He seemed to believe me this time.

I looked at the poor son of a bitch—young enough to be my son, if I'd gotten on with life like nearly everybody else, like Wick and Emily, who had a daughter this boy's age or thereabouts. I wanted to tousle his hair or hug him or recommend a deep cut on an overlooked Dylan album.

"I do, yeah," I said, and then, "Do you sing that old song about hard times?"

"You mean 'Hard Times'?"

"Why, yes, I believe that's the one."

✳

I remember …

"Artesia! Eupora! Lula!" It had begun. Barboro was calling train stops in a mellifluous voice. They all sounded like women's names, and I thought of the one time I almost married, and I thought of Emily, my cousin, and I thought of our young stranger's gal, with her long, pale, tatted gam hanging out the car window …

"Iuka!" I shouted, so loud it was like the train was leaving without me. "Winona! Eden!"

They all looked at me like I'd lost my fucking mind. Even Barboro stopped and seemed to consider it. I hadn't, quite, but they were right, and kind, to wonder, on a night such as this.

✳

I remember, later, sitting alone at the small table up front, staring out the window. I thought of that one woman who walked past before. I imagined us together, far away, walking along with nowhere to go, to be. We'd cross meadows and dells, your odd moor. We'd come upon some flowers. I'd pick one, put it in her hair. It wouldn't stay—her hair too fine for that—but she'd appreciate the gesture. We'd walk on, find ourselves in some small Welsh village, a pub there. We'd go in, have a pint and another. Along about dark, a band of locals would set up in a corner and play their music, miners' ballads and ancient airs. Hard-times music. Sad songs that had lasted, and so maybe we would, too. Later, in the dim of the old place, with us down to the dregs of our beers and the band to the fading notes of its final

40

tune, I'd say to her, "I love you, Gabardine," and she'd say, "Charley, you do say the damnedest things."

*

I only remember bits of the rest of it. I remember looking around for young James Ricketts, but no. Was he out on one of the railroad bridges, the Frisco or the Harahan? I remember thinking I should go for him, save the boy, talk him down from up there. I remember wondering had he already hung or flung himself over the side. But I don't remember what happened next. I only know I didn't go looking.

And I remember stumbling in and out of conversations. I remember feeling like a stray word, alone on a line of type, abandoned by the rest of the sentence, a widow. Or a widower, I guess it would be. I remember feeling like a story that needed to be killed. I may have chanted dirty limericks from atop the bar with my shirt ripped half off.

I remember someone played every Bobby "Blue" Bland record on the jukebox. I pictured him singing those sad songs, standing at the edge of some nightclub stage, knees bent and anguished, eyes closed and bleeding sweat onto his sharkskin suit.

I remember the rat made another appearance. Or it was another rat. This one was rubber, and altogether more handsome and wise than our own. But he was thrown upon the floor and stomped, just the same. It was fun at first but then it turned mean, and then it just sort of petered out. We didn't have the energy to be mean. We'd had too much to drink. We'd been punched too hard. We'd been beaten, and soundly, left to die in a pool of our own piss and vinegar.

But it was a lovely wake, still and all. There were no fights or shots fired. No one was bodily harmed. The last I saw of our earnest young stranger, though, he was in the clutches of one of Madison's ex-wives, all those brown curls disappearing up under her blouse, and her saying, "Come to Floozy." And I

41

remembered that's what Madison called her, Floozy. He always said she was his favorite of all his ex-wives. Well, I heard him say it once.

As for Madison, he slept through most all of it. He looked dead and made up, like the work of Barboro's folks at the mortuary, but for his snoring. He sounded like the Port of Memphis. Nobody paid him much mind, though, stretched out as he was in the back room of the bar, on his bed of sorts. It was a wake, after all. Nobody was in the mood to shoot pool.

∗

And I remember, much later, I tried to call the woman I almost married, years ago. But it was loud in the bar, and I was so very, very drunk. I don't even know what I said. I went on for some time and then stopped. The stilted silence, the awkward pause—the moment, I guess I thought, when she would tell me she had been thinking about me lately, wondering …

But then I only heard a woman's voice I didn't recognize— though sounding, I must say, not all that disinterested.

"And you are?" she said.

"At the bar," I said.

2

# Crystal Shrine Charley among the dead

"How do you feel?"

"I could use the name of a good coroner."

"Oh, it's not as bad as all that."

"Don't you start. I had about all the sunshine and blue skies I could stand from that husband of yours."

"Get up. It's time for breakfast. We can go to Three Little Pigs for biscuits and gravy."

"They're too crowded on Saturdays. I don't want to be around people, so much."

"It's Sunday, Charley. The Lord's day."

"He can have it."

This was at Emily and Wick's house, on Shady Grove in East Memphis. They didn't live in one of the mansions there, but it was a nice place and a tony address—four houses down from the second-richest man in Memphis—so it would do for sleeping off the wake. I don't know how I ended up there, after the wake, but it wasn't the first time. They looked out for me, Emily and Wick, if only for the shit they could give me after—my guardian devils, I called them. But no, not really. They were the best, the both of them.

We were in Emily's writing room. It looked out on the garden and took the morning sun. It seemed a nice day, against the odds. The window was open, and I thought I heard birds. A breeze blew in; the curtains danced and parted. It was like Easter or something out there.

"Christ," I said.

Emily said, "You cuss in your sleep, you know. I've never heard of anybody doing that. You were motherfucking some motherfucker like crazy, there for a while." She said the word like it was the punch line to a slightly off-color nursery rhyme.

"The mouth on you, Emily."

"Then it was women's names. A whole long string of them. Conquests, I suppose."

"Train stops."

"I won't pry."

"What'd you do all this time, sit and listen? Take notes?"

"I read a book and wrote a poem, or the start of one, anyway. It's not any good."

"I don't believe that."

"You think all my poems are good."

"They are."

"I'm the only poet you like, so your judgment's suspect. You don't even like Dylan Thomas."

"The fucking tosspot. He didn't put any kudzu in his poems."

"I don't think there was any kudzu in Wales. And I only put kudzu in the one."

"But it was an awful lot of kudzu."

"An 'awful lot.' You talk like an eight-year-old boy sometimes, Charley." She stood over me, hands on her hips, looking cross. "What do you want to be when you grow up?"

"A newspaper reporter," I said, to her feet, the floor.

I looked up to see what she'd say, but she was gone. Then she was back, with two mugs of coffee.

"Thanks, Em," I said. "You're my favorite cousin."

"Isn't that what Jerry Lee said to Myra Gale?"

I sat up enough on the couch to drink my coffee. She walked across the room and sat at her desk. She walked like she was trying to sneak up on a poem. She was in jeans and some old, white dress shirt of Wick's, the sleeves rolled up. She was barefoot, and ignoring me. She put on her reading glasses and picked up that latest poem of hers. I watched her reading it, the faces she made, little scowls, a slight disagreeable nod. Then something pleased her—or so it seemed, by the way her crow's feet did a little two-step. But then that passed, too. Her eyes were scolding the page now, her own toughest critic, always. I could hardly tell you the color of my own eyes, outside of bloodshot, but hers were hazel.

I sipped my coffee. "Could I trouble you for some sugar," I said, just to be a bother.

She looked over the top of those reading glasses. She flipped me off.

"Ah, never let it be said Cousin Emily won't lift a finger for a poor bastard."

She set down the poem, leaned back in the chair, and put her bare feet up on the desk. I remembered the time, when we were kids and raced barefoot and she won, with those long legs of hers. When I caught up she was at the creek in the woods behind our grandparents' place, a pistol in her hand. She'd found it in the brush. It was cheap-looking and mud-crusted and I didn't figure it would fire, but you never do know.

"Where'd you get that?" I said then.

"Off some mug," she said.

She double-fisted the thing, pointed it at my feet, and said, "Dance, Charley." She'd seen some mug say that to some other mug in a gangster movie, I guessed. Then she made pistol sounds. I stood watching her. She was yellow-haired and tall. She was skinny as rain. She stood there with that pistol, like some movie-girl gangster, saying, "Pow, pow," and I stood watching her, thinking: She's not just faster than me. She's bolder, too. And even if I knew that in a year or two, I'd be faster, and taller, and stronger, she'd always be bolder; there was no catching Cousin Emily at that. So I gave her the most disgusted look I could. I turned to walk away. I wanted to say something, some words to stop a movie-girl gangster where she stood, but no words came. They weren't in me, and I hadn't seen the movie. But no matter. Just by turning and starting to walk, and then walking, I'd dared a girl bolder than me to do the boldest thing there was to be done in that moment.

So she did it.

*Click.*

✳

She stared now out the window, at a bud on a branch, or a bird alighting on a fencepost, or at nothing at all, the air itself. I didn't know, couldn't say. She was writing, I guessed—writing in her mind, how poets do. When I wrote, I always just stared at the keys, in a threatening kind of way. Then I punched them, see.

She looked up over the top of her reading glasses again. "Why are you smiling, Charley?"

"Because I'm lucky, Em. Because I'm the envy of all my friends. This hangover, notwithstanding."

"No, really."

"Oh, you know, thinking of newspaper days. Such times, Em, such times."

"You'll need to move on. Sooner the better."

"Can't I first linger a little in my despair?"

"That would be a nice line for a poem. I may well filch it. But no lingering."

"Can if I want."

"There's that eight-year-old boy again, Charley."

"I do try to keep a hold on my youth, back when all things were possible, outside of beating you in a foot race."

"You still can't."

"It's only on account of this debilitating hangover."

"What did you really want to be when you were a boy, Charley?"

"I wanted to stay a boy. But if I did have to grow up, the hobo life held a certain allure." I wasn't even being a smart-ass.

She said, "You're not even being a smart-ass for once, are you?"

"Nuh-uh."

"Well, good for you. But still. You've got to figure things out, Charley. You're a grown man with too many years left just to piss them away."

"I know. But not just yet, please. Read me that poem of yours, the new one. Just read the start of it, at least. I love to hear you read. You're the poet laureate of my despair."

"It's no good, I told you. It's not even a poem yet. It's just words on a page."

"C'mon, Em."

She flipped me off again, but this time without so much as lifting a finger. Then she read a little of it. She read, *"River rest, river flow. Slow curve of river hips. River tried, river true. Small swell of river belly."*

I about spewed some coffee.

"Emily, are you?"

"Am I what?"

"You know."

"The hell."

"Am I going to be an uncle again?"

"Christ, Charley. It's a poem. They're not all about me. Anyway, I'm forty *or so*. We've got a daughter in college."

"Yeah, and … ?"

She set down her glasses for something to do, and then she looked across the room at me. "I haven't even told Wick yet."

Even she called him Wick; he'd become one of those one-named people, like an Indian chief or fashion designer, I don't know. William 'Wick' Snowden Carr III was his full name. It was a mouthful of the expensive stuff to say it, not that anybody ever did. They just called him what they called his father and grandfather. It's what rich people did. They became known by silly names like Beppy or Pal, because when you live in Art Moderne mansions and summer in France—if summer is, for you, a verb—it's just what you do. At least Wick wasn't a silly name. I'd heard of rich people named Sugsie, Hunkie, and Trow. Last-laugh names, I called them. Because however silly they sound, in the end they're rich and you're not. They have rank and privilege, and you've a cuff in the gutter. Not that I think about or dwell upon such matters, mind you.

"How'd you sniff it out, you bastard?" she said.

I shrugged. "I used to be a reporter," I said, but it wasn't that. I knew her, better than I knew myself or anybody else, better than I knew the capital of North Dakota or who played trumpet on Dylan's "Rainy Day Women #12 & 35." I had, since we were kids. Like how I knew she'd pull the trigger on that pistol, out in the woods, that summer day, even if she didn't know it. I knew she had to. She couldn't *not*.

"Well, keep shut of it for now, you hear me?"

"Yes, ma'am."

So we went for breakfast at Three Little Pigs, a humble little joint over on Quince. The one of us so rich she could afford to be a poet paid. The one of us who didn't have a job or any prospects put up a token fight. I had biscuits and gravy—best in town—and more coffee, and she pushed some eggs around a plate. I watched people reading the Sunday paper like nothing had happened. I'm not going to say it was a little heartbreaking, knowing I didn't have a story in there, that I'd never have one in there again, that after twenty-some-odd years of doing the only thing I ever wanted to do (outside of hoboing, mind you), I had to go and do something else, be somebody else—but it was.

It was heartbreaking as hell.

"Charley, quit scowling at people. It's not their fault."

"They don't even know I exist. I'm not even here."

"That's ridiculous. I can smell you. You're off-gassing like mad. How much did you drink?"

"All of it, Em, every drop."

"Well, it was a wake. Did it help? Was there any, you know, catharsis?"

"I don't believe in the stuff."

"Then why have a wake?"

"To raise one to the gods. To say to them, 'Yeah, you won this round, and the one before, and you'll win the next few. But, you know, fuck you, gods.'"

"The gods must love you, Charley."

"Their boots think I have a nice ass."

"But the wake, really. I've never been to one. Did it help any? Was it fun, or just sad?"

"Sad. But fun, near as I can remember. There was a young stranger there—not one of us. He was a songwriter. He and his girl had a band they called … something, I forget. They were going to play the bar, but the girl ran off."

"Oh, he'll get loads of songs out of that."

"Yeah, that's what I said. The poor bastard."

"Poor bastards write the best songs and the best books and create all the best art. I wouldn't trust a happy man with anything greater than a sandwich."

I sopped the last of my gravy. I snagged an egg from her plate. I was doing a better job of eating for two than she was.

"How do you do it, then?"

"Do what?"

"Write those fierce, lovely poems of yours?"

"Maybe they aren't as fierce and lovely as you think. Or maybe I'm not as happy."

"But you are. Best little family ever was, you and Wick, and lovely Jane away at college, li'l Charley Junior on the way."

"Wick and I fight. Well, not fight, per se. We disagree sometimes, on crucial issues. Well, *issue.*" She leaned forward, confidingly: "Thing is, we have different favorite barbecue joints. It doesn't matter that we agree Three Little Pigs here has the best breakfast of any barbecue joint, and that Tops has the best burger of any barbecue joint. Or even that the Rendezvous has the best sausage and cheese plate of any barbecue joint. That's all settled law. But on the matter of barbecue joint, *sensu stricto,* we battle.

"*Sensu stricto,* huh?"

"It means—"

"I know what it means." I didn't know what it meant, so I asked the names of the barbecue joints in their personal battle royale, though I could make a fair guess.

"It's the Bar-B-Q Shop for me and Central for him."

"Mixed marriage, Memphis-style."

"We make it work."

"I'm a Payne's man, myself."

"Good man."

"But I, you know, eat around."

"Like one does in Memphis."

"Good puzzle would be cross Memphis without passing a barbecue joint."

"Or a church."

We laughed, and then:

"Em?"

"Yeah, Charley?"

"Do you believe in the theory of 'the one'?"

"That there's one person in the world for everybody?"

"Yeah, that."

"Oh, I think there are seven or eight. It's a big world. What about you, Charley?"

"I'd like to think there are at least two."

"You need to get your ashes hauled, Charley."

"Or just scattered," I said.

✳

She dropped the gun. She ran. This was after it went *click,* but alas, not *pow.* She whooshed by me. I was still coming to terms with being alive. I stared at the gun on the ground, and then turned and gave chase. I nearly caught her but didn't quite, with those long legs of hers, and both of us barefoot and cut up from the woods, and too shook, or too something, to say a word about it, ever.

✳

We spent a long day together. Wick was in Nashville. There was talk of opening an office there. He already had one in Little Rock. Seems the consultancy was becoming more of a success than Wick ever intended. It was turning into actual work. He had politicians and Hot New Country singers as clients.

"You could go to work for him," Emily said. "He could use the help."

We were sitting on a stone bench in Memorial Park Cemetery, on Poplar. We'd gone to see Emily's mother, my aunt. I guessed Emily was telling her she was pregnant. I could just see the look on her mother's face. Or the mask, more like. She was a puzzle, always kept it inside—the polar opposite of her sister, my mother.

"What's he do, just talk to people? I'd hate that."

"He listens, too. It's, you know, the whole range of human interaction."

"Ugh." I sounded more than ever like that eight-year-old boy; I might have been staring at a plate of sprouts, or a pretty girl.

"He says it's easy. He says his clients almost always know what the answer is. They just need to hear it from somebody who won't take any shit from them—sorry, Mother. They've had some minor scandal, usually. Maybe some Hot New Country singer's been caught in public with his pants down or her dress up—one time, *his* dress was up. That was a thing. Or it's booze or pills, you know. Doesn't matter. Wick says the answer's always the same, pretty much—just come right out and admit whatever you've done, say you're sorry as can be, you weren't raised that way, and it won't happen again. Don't stall and don't lie and don't hedge and don't say somebody slipped something in your drink, even if somebody slipped something in your drink. That's what he tells them all. He says a trained parrot could do it."

"You're saying I could be a trained parrot?"

"No, you're right—you couldn't be trained, at this point."

"Maybe I could open a rival consultancy, next door to Wick's. I'd advise people to stall and lie and hedge and say somebody slipped something in their drink, even if they didn't. We always liked it better when people did all that—sold more newspapers that way. It became a whole week's worth of stories instead of just a day or two."

"Such a noble profession, newspapers."

I said, "Wick's not dispensing that advice to be noble. He just knows what works. He doesn't insist on them being sorry, right? They just need to say it and have people believe it. And people want to believe. They're trusting, by nature. They're hopeful. Anyway, if Wick's clients are politicians and country singers, well, they're all just performers. They can sell a lie."

"He never claimed it's noble. He's just getting people out of the fix they're in, fast as he can. It's a service. He wanted to call his consultancy 'The Fix-It Shop,' but—"

"Don't tell me. Let me guess. Oh, this is good. Some consultant told Wick he needed to call his consultancy something a little more serious."

She smiled. "Something like that."

"Don't they have consultants in Nashville already? Hard to imagine those Music City slickers taking advice from anybody with Shelby County plates. They hate us."

"Yeah, that's what I thought, too. But there's a Memphis expat over there, high up at one of the record labels. He called Wick, told him those Nashville consultants tend to want to show how smart they are, when all you need's some good country sense."

"You'd think they'd have good country sense, in the capital of country music and all."

"Have you listened to what they've been calling country music, the last few decades?"

"Hell, woman, what do I know? I think Hot New Country's Lefty Frizzell and them."

She sang a little of "Always Late (With Your Kisses)." I'd forgotten she could sing, too. Damn her. Damn her voice and damn her eyes. Damn those long legs and that small swell of river belly.

I stood and said, "Well, how about I give you some time with your mother? You can tell her what her favorite nephew sniffed out already."

I went walking through the cemetery. My parents weren't there—they were in a couple of urns in a shed out back of my house, in a box marked "Keep—or not." (But I'd kept them, hadn't I?) I wandered around, looking for famous dead people. Sam Phillips was there somewhere. I couldn't find him, but I did stumble on Isaac Hayes. They invented themselves, those two, Sam and Isaac. They became who they wanted be, made the world look, made it listen. Isaac's grave marker was golden with images of him—Isaac as Black Moses, Isaac around a piano writing songs like "Soul Man," Isaac as a movie star with gun pulled (don't get a lot of that in cemeteries where you live, eh?), Isaac as family man. Neighboring Isaac's grave, just by one of those coincidences Memphis manages in its sleep, was the grave of another dead musician, a punk rocker who went by the name Jay Reatard and sang such songs as "Feeling Blank Again" and "It Ain't Gonna Save Me." He wasn't my thing, but I'd heard him called a genius. He played a white Gibson Flying V guitar and was buried with it, apparently. There were bronze guitars and musical notes on his marker, and these words: "Memphis Punk Rocker." I can't imagine aspiring to more, can you?

Charlie Rich was there, too, somewhere. I couldn't find him, but he was. Now, Charlie, he was different. I believe Sam Phillips said Charlie Rich had more talents than any of those cats who came through Sun Studio, excepting only Howlin' Wolf. Think of it. More than Elvis and Johnny Cash and Jerry Lee Lewis, more than B.B. King, and my personal favorite, Little Junior Parker. I think Charlie had too many talents. He loved to sing jazz, loved to croon for you, "Mood Indigo" and the like, but he could sell pretty country records like a proper fool, and so he got tugged all sorts of ways. He got chewed up a little by the business. He made a lot of money and he drank too much and one time, at a country music awards show, when it came time for him to announce the entertainer of the year or some such, he took the card out of the envelope, and his cigarette lighter out of his pocket, and lit the thing as he read the winner's name: John Denver. I don't know if some consultant told him to apologize later. I hope to hell not but probably so.

I couldn't find the great Charlie Rich, but I did come across a real-life female outlaw named Laura Bullion. I remembered reading something about her once—how she robbed banks and trains with Butch Cassidy and the Wild Bunch, how she did time and passed as a man and went by many names, including "Rose of the Wild Bunch" and "The Thorny Rose." I told her there was a woman she just had to meet. I said they'd be fast friends. "But no bank jobs, just now," I said. "She's with child."

Then I wandered over to the Crystal Shrine Grotto. It's another of those only-in-Memphis places. It's a sort of man-made cave filled with religious tableaus, I guess you'd call them—the life of Jesus, all the big holy to-dos. I know, I know: Sounds like a place teenagers would go to smoke dope. I find the place kind of spooky, myself, not at all conducive to deep thought or spiritual oneness or career planning. So I went in.

There was a young couple in there, Japanese tourists. I think he'd just asked her to marry him, or they were having a fight, one. They both looked at me like maybe I'd want to officiate. I shrugged, and he said something to her in Japanese. She punched him in the shoulder, a hard jab for such a slight girl. It rocked him. She turned and stormed out. She was all in black, shoes and socks and jeans and a Sun Studio T-shirt, but for her hair, which was pink, in a nice touch, I thought, if only for visibility. She walked like she had some other boyfriend to go and hit. She walked like she wouldn't stop until she hit the shores of home— the rising sun had best watch itself. She walked like a right jab. We both watched her go and then we looked at each other. He said—well, how in hell do I know? I shrugged and he did, too. Then he reached in his shirt pocket and pulled out a joint. I said, "I don't smoke, but you and Crystal Shrine Jesus go ahead."

I met back up with Emily. I asked what her mother had to say about the baby.

"She didn't say much," Em said.

"She never did," I said. "What about Wick? You worried about telling him? You holding off?"

"Nah. You know Wick. He'll be thrilled. He always wanted more kids. And for some damned reason I've never been able to explain, the man thinks everything I do is just fine."

"It's more than Wick who thinks it."

"He's the only one who has to live with me."

"You've got the best husband," I said. "He adores you."

We stood under an old oak, next to a grave for a woman named Hattie and another named Hester. They were sisters, both lived to just shy of ninety. A few feet away were a husband and wife, with the improbable B-movie names of Mack and Doll. I bet they had some times, those two. And there was a woman named Early and a man named Tipsy and another whose inscription read "Beloved Papa." There were soldiers from our sundry wars, and I remembered a story I wrote for the newspaper about one who survived the war but came home shy an arm. It was his good one, the right, so out of bitterness and gall he decided he'd be the best left-handed son of a bitch in this cursed world at something. I think maybe he had in mind something like sport fishing down in the Gulf, but hell, in the end, it was just drinking. He was so good at it, it killed him. It was a story about what war does to men, and men to fifths of whiskey. I'd go see him, even after I'd written the story—something I never did. We'd watch war movies together. (If only my father could see me, I thought. If only.) He'd get drunk and riled up and wave his one good arm during the pivotal battles. Piece of work, Big Bill Fee. He was buried over in West Tennessee, where he was born. Had a flag-draped casket and all. I went over for the funeral. Not for another story. Just to go, to be there. That night I went home and raised a drink to the man, right-handed. I don't know that I cried, but it's entirely possible.

I meandered on. I looked around one last time for Charlie Rich. There was another story about him I remember hearing. This, too, was when he was a big country star. This was when he was drinking a lot. He'd sung the anthem before a big football game at Liberty Bowl stadium. He'd showed up stewed then, too, and had an awful time with the old tune. I like to think he sang it to the melody of "Mood Indigo" or his own "Don't Put No Headstone on My Grave," but he probably just butchered it, as happens with bad singers trying too hard or good ones too stewed. Afterward, he was riding up the elevator to the press box to watch the game. Elvis was on the elevator, too, football fan that he was. There was a sportswriter in there, too. He told the story to another sportswriter, who told it to me. The elevator started up and Elvis looked at Charlie and smiled and said, "That song ain't no 'Behind Closed Doors,' is it, Charlie?" And Charlie, he just said, "Fuck you, Elvis."

I hadn't noticed Emily standing beside me, but there she was. She elbowed me and then we started back to the car.

"You need to find some woman to adore, Charley," she said. "If you adore her, and she can just about tolerate you, well, that ought to be enough to make a marriage."

"You think?"

"Sure. Women like to be adored. Men like to be tolerated."

"The bastards."

I thought of my father beating my mother, my mother giving him hell back. I thought of the brooding and the seething in that house. It was like thunder and lightning turned on each other.

I thought of the young Japanese couple, and wondered whether they'd get back together and get married, if she would vow to rule, and him to obey.

I thought of Crystal Shrine Jesus, who died for … what, exactly?

We stood at the car.

"Well, I am quite the catch," I said. "Man of leisure, envy of all my friends."

"You? Friends?"

"I've got you—"

"I'm family. I don't count."

"Oh, you count. And there's Wick—"

"I'll give you Wick."

"And—" I didn't pause for dramatic effect. I paused to think. "See?"

"Well, you know. My dear friends at the newspaper. Ol' Stell, and Mad. Flippen, of course. Barboro, poor bastard. Vollintine—he was all right, for an editor. I even like one photographer—Arthur Pearl, good man. And there's—ah, shit."

"What, Charley?"

"Jesus Christ on a fucking railroad bridge—the kid!"

# All that glitters is broken glass

So we went looking for young James Ricketts. I'd forgotten all about the poor bastard.

Emily drove to the river. She drove down Poplar to Union, Union to downtown. She worked her way to the interstate, the old bridge there, the Memphis & Arkansas. They call it the old bridge because there's a new bridge, the Hernando DeSoto—well, not new, but only forty-odd years old. Contemporaries, us. Nobody'd called me new in a very long time.

"You don't really believe he'd—"

"No, surely no. But, still. Hell, I don't know, Em. Romantic notions of the young and all."

"You make him sound like a poet, not an ink-stained wretch."

"He's young but with an old soul, and a rare gift. Plus, he wrote that story about the guy who was about to jump off the Frisco but was talked down."

"So?"

"It might have given him ideas."

"I read that story. He had a nice touch. But maybe he identified more with the cop who talked the man down."

"I don't think so. I know him."

"So you two were close?"

"I wouldn't say close," I said. "You know me."

"But close enough to know his mind, to think he might really do it. Close enough to care."

"That last one, I guess."

"And you think, if he really had a mind to jump, he'd still be up there, two days later, doing what ... trying to work up the nerve? Waiting for somebody to come and talk him down?"

"I know I would."

"That's not a romantic notion, Charley. That's just being chickenshit."

"We work with what we have."

She took the old bridge to Arkansas, the two railroad bridges to our right. She drove as slowly as she could, with all the eighteen-wheelers roaring by. I kept watch.

"See any jumpers?"

"No jumpers that I can see."

She crossed into Arkansas, all that nothing there, and turned around. She took the first exit back on the Memphis side.

"This is ridiculous, Charley."

"It is."

"He's probably just sleeping off a bender, you know."

"He wasn't at the wake."

"Some people aren't social drinkers. They're solitary ones."

"Drink makes you social. Anyway, it was a wake."

"Meaning?"

"It's like a funeral, for Christ's sake. There's a moral, ethical responsibility to attend."

"A moral, ethical responsibility to drink your face off?"

"Sometimes you have to sink to the moment."

"Well, he's young. He probably has his own crowd. He probably has a girlfriend. He's probably all up in her arms, or her something, as we speak."

She smiled. I laughed.

"I know, you're right. This is ridiculous, like you say. Waste of time. Sorry."

"But we're here."

"Right. Might as well look a little more, yeah."

We tried Crump Park and Martyrs Park and we tried this unmarked little road that took us down into the shadows of the railroad bridges. It was remote down there, a little dark even in daylight. It could have been a drug drop, or some hobo picnic ground. We got out and sat on the hood.

I looked at the graffiti on some of the low beams. I saw the words "I love …" but you couldn't read the next word. I looked down to ground level. There was a right-turn sign just ahead of us, with "CRIPS" written in silver across the black arrow. The sign had been ill-treated by time, the elements, man, and perhaps some large river creature come up from the depths of Big Muddy. It was bent, mangled, stained, and knocked woozy. I noticed every nick in the thing, as if I had to go back to the office and describe it in a story. Old habits. Fucking fuck me. I sighed.

"What was it about reporting, Charley?" Like she was reading my mind. She always could do that.

"The puzzle, you know. Putting it all together. That was part of it. Going out and getting all the pieces—the pieces of whatever mess somebody had created. That's usually what the stories were, a mess of somebody's making. There were a million little pieces, in disarray, and they had to be made sense of. All that glitters is broken glass—an old reporter told me that once. So I'd go out there and start my gathering. One thing would lead to another. One person to another. I'd talked to them—listened, mostly. I'm a good listener."

"Lost art."

"Then I'd have all the pieces in hand. I'd have all I needed. Then came my favorite part. I could hole up and write—not be bothered, talked to. It was, in its way, the hardest part, to bring order to all you'd gathered, to distill it, to communicate in a way that was fair and interesting and maybe even had a sort of a sixth-grade grace to it. This thing I'd create, Em. Tommy Miles told me one time, they're like building houses. And they are. Some are cottages or bungalows, and sometimes you get a crack at a castle. But you build each one just so, no matter the size. You built it tight. You make it plumb. Because every story is important, in its way. The story, Em. That's what I lived for—coming back to the office and disappearing into my hole and writing my way out of it. It felt that way. I might as well have been in one. I wasn't aware of anything going on around me. I didn't hear anybody, talk to anybody. I was happiest then."

"You'll be happy again, Charley, just doing something else, is all."

"But I don't want to do anything else. Hell, I'm not even sure I want to be happy anymore."

We watched a barge pass by on the river. I tried to read the name on the tug. Some woman's name, no doubt. I wondered if I could make it as a deck hand. Lots of toting and lifting, I supposed, taking orders. You'd have to know all the knots. Maybe I could remember how to tie a bowline and two half-hitches from my Boy Scout days. But hell, I hardly knew them when I was a Tenderfoot. All I wanted at that age was to daydream stories and draw little comic books and do whatever Cousin Emily was doing.

I followed the barge until it disappeared. I closed my eyes and imagined Mark Twain out there, on a raft on the river, relaxing and telling tales, smoke and calliope tunes pouring from his pipe. He was comfortable in his skin and bones, and that trademark white suit of his. He was at ease in the world. He stood and stretched and then sat back down. He looked on the short side, actually. Most great writers were—Twain, Faulkner, Fitzgerald. Hell, Proust could have been a jockey, he was so short. He lived in a shoebox. Nah, just fucking with you.

I opened my eyes, looked up at the railroad bridges. They were the color of rust and midnight and train smoke. They were side by side. The Frisco was older. It was considered something of a wonder when it was built in the late 1800s. It was the first bridge to cross the Lower Mississippi, and was known, for a while, as the Great Bridge. The Harahan came along some twenty years later and served its purpose without need for such pomp.

"But one's as good as the other for jumping, I suppose," I said, as if Emily was still up there in my mind, reading the thing.

"We talking about young James Ricketts?"

"We are."

"Whom you barely even know."

"Yes, cousin. Whom I barely even know."

"But you did at least try to call him."

"Um. Don't have his number."

"Went by his house?"

"Again, um. Don't know where he lives."

"Charley, you two ever talk? You and James Ricketts?" I shrugged in that disarming way men do. Four parts sheepishness to two parts shame, to one part eight-year-old boy.

"Not a conversation, per se," I said. "Always meaning to. I read his stuff, watched him work. He'd do like me, gather up all he needed for the story, then come back to the office, hunker down, hole up. Sat there at his keyboard, hunched like a very old man. Didn't speak to a soul until he was done with the thing. Boy had talent, instincts, social ineptitude. All the tools. He loved it, you could tell. He wasn't like the other young ones. So that one time, after that one story, the one about the jumper, I sort of nodded at him."

"What did he do?"

"He sort of grinned."

"Ah, the human connection," she said, "sort of," and then: "You saw yourself in him. Or you saw yourself as a father figure to him. Something like that, Charley?"

"Given as how I pretty much ignored the boy, never gave him an actual word of encouragement or guidance, I'd say it must have been a father figure, yep."

I shrugged and she rolled her eyes. We sat there on the car hood a little while longer. We sat there taking in the view. "Are you mad at me, Emily?"

"Only furious." But she smiled when she said it. "The view's nice, anyway."

She pushed off the hood, walked a few steps. She stopped and stretched.

"There's another side you can see," I said, "like waving to yourself."

"What'd you say, Charley?"

"From that one poem of yours, about rivers. About how you prefer them to oceans."

"That was ages ago. I always wondered what it was about."

"Or else it was about sex. Most poems are, aren't they?"

"It's blues songs you're thinking of."

"Oh, right. I'm just a newspaperman, you know. Or an ex one. All newspaper stories are about is fifteen column inches of more or less basic, builder-grade fact. That's it and no more."

"Poems are about half a dozen things. There's God, death, chance, memory, the whole rivers vs. oceans debate. And sex, of course."

"And longing."

"Longing is the blues, too."

"So that's what I've got. The blues. And here I thought it was languor."

"Languor, Charley?"

"I just wanted to say the word."

We watched another tug pass. I couldn't make out the name of that one, either.

"We might as well go," I said. "He's not here."

"You sound disappointed."

I didn't know if I'd been trying to talk myself into something, or out of it. Had I wanted to find young James, straddling some rusted beam of big iron, distraught, about to do the thing? So I could go and save him, talk him down? So then we could be friends—friends that talk and share things, the older a mentor to the young? Father figure? Really?

She started the car.

"What are you thinking, Charley? You have that look you get."

Romantic notions of the old, I thought.

"Nothing," I said.

✳

She drove me home. I got out of the car and then turned and leaned in the window.

"It's not that I don't have a plan, you know."

"I know."

"I *had* a plan. It was a damned good one. I'd be a reporter. I'd be that all my life."

"So use those skills of yours, Charley, if they haven't gotten rusty in the couple of days since you were fired. Find the young you. Find James Ricketts, make sure he's all right. Talk to him. Tell him you're there for him. Tell him life's a son of a bitch, but he'll come through. Tell him to buck up."

"I'll do that. I will."

"And buck up, yourself. Get a new plan. You *get* to be somebody else now. Who gets to do that?"

I started up the walk. I turned away and then back.

"I don't want to be anything else, Em."

She just stared back. "Don't make me shoot you again, Charley."

She laughed and I did, too—but both of us a little shocked, I think. It was the first time either of us had mentioned that day in the woods. Thirty years on, and we'd talked about everything in the world but that.

"You didn't shoot me."

"I tried."

"Well."

So we were talking about it now. We were joking but we were talking about it.

"I like to think I'd have missed."

"You, at such close range? Nah, not you, Stagger Emily. You'd have hit me square."

"You'd have died, and they'd have sent me to girl prison, and then where would we be?"

"I'd be under a tree at Memorial Park, taking guitar lessons on the Flying V from Jay Reatard, and writing songs with Charlie Rich and Isaac Hayes."

"Oh, sure. Swell for you, fella. But what about me in girl prison?"

"Ah, you'd have busted out, first day. Jimmy a lock or shimmy out some chute or other."

We laughed again. I turned and started back up the walk. There was more to say but we didn't say it. She might have said that day in the woods, finding that gun, pointing it at me, telling me to dance, pulling the trigger, saying "pow," was what made her want to be a poet. That was always my theory. It was right after that, at least, she began to write. I think she was trying to understand herself, explain herself. So it had to happen. It was necessary. She had to pull the trigger. She couldn't *not*.

I turned back but I didn't say all that. I didn't say anything. Anyway, I needed it to happen, too. I had a theory on that, as well: It's what made me want to be a reporter. It's what opened my eyes to the world. It's when I first noticed the details.

I came to the end of the walk. I stopped at the stoop. Home. My little Midtown bungalow. It wasn't a tony address and the second-richest man didn't live four houses down, though I did have a neighbor who claimed he was an extra in that great Memphis movie, "Mystery Train," and got to meet Joe Strummer. Even the professional skeptic in me wanted to believe it was so.

I stood there at the stoop. I looked down and saw them— two days of newspapers lying there. Those fucking things.

I about tossed them into the shrubs, but then I thought again of poor young James Ricketts. Was he the jumpy type? Nah, surely not. Not bright young James. But still.

I sat on the stoop and started paging through those papers, looking for falling bodies and other sad tales.

# Gutters and funny shoes

I didn't have a number for him and I didn't know where he lived. I didn't know his friends; I didn't know if he had any. He didn't go out and drink with us. That's practically the only time I ever talked to anybody else.

I called Flippen but Flippen's wife said Flippen was asleep. I said it was three o'clock in the afternoon of a Sunday and she said, "Did you think I was going tell you he was still at church, Charley?"

I called Barboro. He said young James lived downtown, a loft there, when he'd started at the paper. But he moved to a house somewhere. Midtown, maybe?

"You think he'd do anything crazy, Will?"

"You mean like trying to get another fucking newspaper job?"

We laughed. I asked how the hell he was. He said, "Life after death's no big thing, Charley. Look at the both of us. We're still here. You know what's hard?" I asked him what. "Bowling," he said. I asked if he'd been hanging out at Billy Hardwick's All Star Lanes since we'd been let go and he said, "No, I'm just saying. I just mean—hell, I don't know." I said I knew, though I didn't, quite. Bowling probably was a metaphor for life, if you want to look into it. It's all gutters and funny shoes, isn't it? I looked down at my own, but they were far too drab to attempt the dread seven-ten split. And my socks didn't match, as ever.

I said, "Well, OK then, Will." I asked if he thought young James might have thrown himself off the Frisco or the Harahan. There was a pause on the phone, and then Barboro said, "I think he might still be in line up there." I waited for a small laugh, something. It liked to never come, and then it did. I said, "God help us." He said there might be a line for that, too.

I didn't call anybody else just then. They might have answered, and I was weary of human interaction. I took off driving the streets of Midtown, not so much looking for signs of James Ricketts, but to think.

I drove as far east as Highland and as far west as Danny Thomas. I drove by the newspaper and then back and then yet again and it was only on the last pass that I summoned the fortitude to not flip it off. I felt a little like my inner eight-year-old was now a fresh fifteen and impertinent as hell. It was the best I'd felt in days. Fifteen years old—maybe I could get a paper route.

I drove by Payne's Bar-B-Q on Lamar, not because I thought young James Ricketts might have been in there having a pork shoulder sandwich but because I thought I might need one. But I forgot the place was closed Sundays. Or I forgot it was Sunday. I wondered if it would be like this, the days all running together. I ended up in the Cooper-Young district. There were people eating in restaurants and drinking in bars and buying books at the bookstore. I went in the record store around the block, thinking young James might have been a regular there. I remembered he'd written a story for the paper about people buying vinyl again. He'd have known the store. I was a bit of an old record fiend myself—not because I'd rediscovered vinyl but because I'd never abandoned it. Just one more example of my clinging to the old, I supposed. Wick would tell me I should visit the modern world sometime, and bask in its splendors. The way Wick described the modern world it sounded like a cross between the Louvre, outer space, and one of those restaurants that served red onion compote. I said I was fine with my old records and my old self. Wick said the world was changing and would leave me behind, and we both knew he was right. It was coming to pass. And so what was I going to do about it? That was a question for another day. I was looking for young James Ricketts.

"Do you have a customer who"—how the hell could I describe somebody as nondescript as young James?—"well, young guy—"

"Keep going, I think I can picture him."

The clerk knew me a little. I don't think they had many middle-aged fuckers as customers, and I'd buy everything they got in by Junior Parker. I said, "Well, you know those hipster hats the hipsters all wear these days?" The clerk said yeah. I said, "Well, he doesn't wear one. And he doesn't wear anything else hipsters wear. He doesn't dress like anybody at all who's trying to be stylish or fashionable or—"

He looked at me, as if to say, *Kinda like you, then?* Then he said it, and added, "Only younger."

Fair play to the smart arse. I said, "All right, then. Yeah."

"What's he listen to? That's really how we know people. We honestly don't pay attention to what they wear." He leaned across the counter and whispered, though it was only one other person in the store, and she was in the back, listening to an old record. "But don't tell the hipsters."

I said I didn't know what he listened to. I said I guessed I was his friend but apparently not a good one. I said we worked together at the newspaper, but they'd let us go.

The clerk said something about how that was a damned shame and what poor bastards we were. I'll tell you what a damned shame is, good people—when a music store clerk bemoans the sad state of *your* industry.

The girl in the back of the store had headphones on. They had a record player back there so you could listen before you bought. She started to dance a little, a skinny-white-girl slink. Cigarette smoke in a dress. It was like an old-woman's shift, a thrift-store thing, but she wore it with Army-looking boots, unlaced. They were too big for her feet and clanked as she danced.

The clerk said, "The Soul Children."

I looked at him and then realized he was guessing, that it was a game the clerks played. I watched the girl dance some more—sinuous, I believe, was the word for it. I thought she might come all up out of those boots and just float about the room. I said, "Ann Peebles. That song about breaking up somebody's home."

He nodded and smiled. He was lost there for a bit then, suddenly listening to Ann Peebles in his head and watching that skinny girl dance in the back of the store.

"James Ricketts," I said.

"Huh?"

"That's the young guy I'm looking for."

He came out of it. "Jimmy?" he said.

"Well, I guess."

"Yeah, yeah. He comes in. Jimmy, sure. Hunts for old Black gospel 45s. The Hightower Brothers and the Trumpet Sounds, like that."

"Has he been in lately? Since Friday?"

"I don't know. I didn't work Saturday. He might have. Something happen to him? Besides losing his job, I mean?"

"Well, no. I don't know. Hope not. I just wanted to check on him, you know, make sure he's all right."

"Well, I were you, I'd just go see him. He lives over on Polk, out back of the main house on the corner. I gave him a ride home one night last week. He was my last customer."

"Well, damn," I said. "Thanks, I guess, for getting around to telling me that. Let's hope he hasn't jumped off the Frisco or Harahan in the meantime."

"Jump off a railroad bridge? Jimmy? Nah, man, I doubt that shit."

I was turning to leave when the girl brought up the record to buy. I looked at the clerk and he looked at me. He said to her, "So what you got?"

She held up an Ann Peebles album, *I Can't Stand the Rain*, from 1974 on Hi Records. Ann's face was on the cover, in profile. It wasn't the album with the song about breaking up somebody's home, but it had "I'm Gonna Tear Your Playhouse Down," my other favorite of hers, and "A Love Vibration," and of course the title song.

The clerk said, "Ann Peebles," kind of dreamy-like, and we started to lose him again for a second. You could almost hear the music playing in his head again, Ann singing, the horns swaying, that famous Hi Rhythm section holding it down and lifting it up, all at once. Watching him hand that record back to her, gently but almost grudgingly, and her taking it, almost haltingly but with both hands out, it was like that record was a religious totem or controlled substance, and I was privy to something secret, sacred. I found myself taking down every detail, a reporter again, if only for those few seconds.

The girl got to the door and stopped. She raised that record up out of the bag and gave that cover a kiss, knocked it a slow one. Then she was gone.

I felt a little better then about the youth of America, to know the deep and subtle intricacies of soul music were still being taught in the home. Good girl, well raised.

I spent a few more minutes in the store, perusing the used albums. I bought an old Mud Boy & the Neutrons record, the one with "Land of 1000 Shotguns (Part 2)." Outside, I turned the car around and drove a couple of blocks and found it, no problem. I went out back of the main house.

I knocked on the door. No answer.

Then I gave it a proper bang.

"James," I said.

"Jimmy," I shouted.

# Requiem for the wreck of me

I was about to turn and go. I didn't know where. Then he came to the door, seeming disheveled, half apart. Looking at him, it hit me for the first time that he was named for a disease, or a childhood bone defect, whatever. His name had that second, silent "t," but still. It was like being named Billy Scurvy or something. Damn—Billy Scurvy. You'd about have to go into punk rock with a name like that, just to get a date. Maybe James Ricketts had it as bad.

"Charley, what's wrong?" he said to me.

"I'm checking on you, James," I said.

He'd only just opened the door enough to stick his head out. He was shirtless, his hair a mess. He was a skinny thing. Pale, too. All the young people seemed so skinny these days. I wanted to round them up and take them out for ribs and real beer, tell them to quit being so goddamn wan. I looked at him. I heard music in the background—vintage Black gospel. One of those old 45s from the record store. Some raw, righteous stuff. What you'd play on a Sunday if you were trying to decide whether to stick around for Monday. Ah, the poor, young bastard. It was one of those records where the lead singer sounded like a pissed-off preacher and the backup singers sounded like a sweet choir of angels. It was hard to be heard over the sound of them all.

"I'm here for you, James."

I'd never really been *there* for anybody. I didn't know what it entailed, exactly, didn't know what came next. Maybe we could just kind of be there for each other.

"What do you mean, Charley?"

"I've been worried, since they sacked us. I thought you might—"

"Thought I might what?"

We were almost shouting, the both of us.

"Do you think you could turn the music down? We could talk? I could come in—"

His eyes flashed inside and then back at me.

"Hold on a sec. I'll be right out."

So I milled around outside. I looked around the grounds. James Ricketts lived in what must have been designed as an artist's studio. It was a shack, really, about the size of a studio apartment, with a window unit. But nice, as shacks go. It was painted a shade of yellow just slightly funkier than egg yolk.

I looked elsewhere about the yard. It was a well-kept place—the main house was painted powder blue, with white, Christmas-style lights strung all around the little front porch. There was some yard art I couldn't explain or interpret, spaced about the grounds, and a rusted swing set that might have been from some previous owner. I didn't see any deck chairs or wrought-iron rockers where we might sit and talk.

James Ricketts finally appeared, in an old white T-shirt and jeans. He was barefoot.

"What's this all about, Charley?"

"Can we sit down?"

We looked around. There was nothing but the swing set.

I didn't know why we couldn't just go in James's house. Maybe it was littered with empty bottles and pills and all manner of filth. Maybe he'd given up, and those vintage Black gospel records were the only thing keeping him alive. But, hell, it had only been since Friday that we'd been sacked. The young, though; you know, they're not stalwart, like us old fuckers.

"We could just sit in your place, James," I said.

"It's small," he said. "It's a mess. You know."

So he shrugged and led us over to the swing set. He sat down on one swing. Rail-thin as he was, he fit just fine. I sat in the swing next to him. It was a little snug for me. I felt like the fat kid on the playground, eight years old again. I expected some brats to burst from the bushes and start beating the shit out of me. I expected my father to stick his mug out the back door of the main house and glare at me for being me.

"So how the hell are you, James? We didn't see you at the wake."

"I don't drink, Charley."

"Not a drop?"

"A little wine, is all. But no, not really."

"Well, see, that's one reason I was worried."

James smiled. He was twenty-three, twenty-four, looked seventeen. He was smart, with a quick wit, for a kid—the kind of wit that flies over other kids but impresses adults; the kind that's dangerous for a kid to have, if he wants to fit in and not have the shit beaten out of him on a semi-regular basis. But best of all, you could see him learning, growing wise, before your eyes. He listened, was the thing. With his eyes, he listened. He knew he didn't know it all. He wasn't fully formed. You could almost hear him growing—the creak and stretch of him, the groan of his bones. He was naturally curious. He would have made somebody a good son, but he'd have been even a better reporter. I just knew it.

"How do you mean?" But then it came to him. He grinned a little. "Oh, I see, Charley. You mean, if a newspaperman who's just been fired, who's vulnerable, at his wit's end, doesn't fill himself with every ounce of mood-altering chemical depressant he can possible hold, why, there's no telling what might come of him, what harm he might cause to himself or others."

"And here I thought I was going to have to explain it to you."

Now young James Ricketts pushed off with his bare feet and began to swing like it was sixth-grade recess or something.

He was a sight. It wasn't that he was like an overgrown boy but rather some ungainly bird not yet prepared for flight. Maybe he never would be. He had long skinny feet—awful looking flappers, if you want to know the truth of it, with toes long as fingers, more like claws than anything. But good for swinging, it turned out. They dug into the dirt, despite the dirt being hard-baked by the Memphis sun and long ignored by any Midtown tykes. The claws dug in and those long legs of his did their limber thing, they bent easily and at odd angles and worked together, and he achieved a sort of wheezy grace. The old swing set, rusty as it was, made a sort of woozy music as he sort of soared.

I watched, watcher that I was. Then young James Ricketts said, "C'mon, Charley."

So I pushed off. I got some momentum going. My swing was cursing me, by the sound of it. The whole swing set was. I smiled as I sort of soared. We did that for a while. Not talking, just swinging, and then I realized I was swinging and he wasn't. I wondered if he thought he was saving me now.

"Here's the thing, James," I said when I stopped. "I'm sorry as hell I never paid you much attention at the paper. That's my fault. I'm not really much for, you know, people. You may have noticed. But the fact of it is, I thought you were a serious young newspaperman—a good one, the best of all the young ones we had, the only one who didn't think he already knew every damned thing. You struck me, honestly, as the only one of them I expected to still be doing it in ten, twenty, thirty years—if newspapers lasted that long. Which they won't."

"Thank you, Charley." He seemed about to reach over and pat me on the shoulder, but there were two strands of swing-set chain between us. I think both of us were glad of it.

"I saw myself in you," I said. "A young me in young you. I saw you as a real newspaperman. I didn't figure you wanted to be anything else. I didn't figure you *could* be anything else. Like me, that you were born, made, wired, whatever, to be this one thing. And here you are, twenty-three, twenty-four—and look seventeen—and the business is dying. Not just here. Everywhere, all over. We're fucked, see. Me. You. Us."

He leaned forward in his swing, then turned in and looked at me. "You thought I was going to kill myself, Charley?"

"I kind of had it all worked out. It would be one of the railroad bridges. Frisco or the Harahan. I'd written the lede of the story, in my head. Then, you know, I went looking for you."

The lad seemed at a loss. He didn't know whether to laugh or hug me. Just then the door of his little house opened.

"Jimmy, you coming or what?" A young woman's voice.

Jimmy turned and looked over at her. He waved and grinned. She grinned and waved back. She only just stuck her head out the door, as James had done. She was fair-haired and pretty. They fit—you could see it, straight off. Just from the little I could see, she had that same disheveled, half-apart look I'd seen in James, and then I realized, thick me.

"James, when I came knocking, were you two in there having carnal relations to vintage Black gospel music on a Sunday?"

He stood. I tried to, but got stuck in the swing. He helped me out.

He smiled, all sheepish.

"Emily was right, as always," I said.

"Who's Emily?"

"Oh, friend. Cousin, actually. She said you'd be—well, were you?"

A hand on my shoulder.

"I think the greater sin would be to talk about it, don't you, Charley?"

"Good man, James."

"Call me Jimmy. My friends do."

We shook hands.

"Friends, yeah."

"Just between us friends, though, I can't believe you thought I'd jump off a bridge—"

"Jump or hang yourself, one. I was leaving it open."

"—but the fact that you cared enough. The things you said."

"I meant them."

"I know you did."

"But don't you feel, I don't know, devastated?"

"The thing is, Charley, I'd only been at the paper for a year. Not long enough to even call myself a real reporter, much less to say I'd found my calling. I don't even know if I was any good. Just that I felt myself getting better."

"But the way you worked at it. Cared enough to try to get better. Studied the craft."

"That's just me, Charley. I throw myself into things. I just do. And the newspaper, I'm not sure it ever felt like the place I wanted to spend the rest of my days. It felt more like—how to say this?—a better version of college. Real-world grad school, where I could learn skills I could take anywhere. Study masters at work, like you, Charley. Like Tommy Miles and Stell. Jesus, those two. I always studied my stories the next morning in the paper, and the ones they edited were miraculously better in little ways I barely understood. Sometimes I couldn't even tell what had been changed, what words deleted or phrases smoothed. I'm not saying magic, but. Kind of a laying on of the hands."

"Precise as watchmakers, those two," I said. "Their fingers, like little wands they waved over the keys."

"I thanked Tommy Miles one day. For what he'd done to my story the day before. He looked up and smiled and said, 'Oh, Comma Boy.'"

I smiled.

"I asked him if I used too many or not enough, and he said, 'Yes.' I said, 'Both, you mean?' 'Yes.' I asked it if was somehow possible, to use too many commas and not enough, all at once?"

"What did our man say?"

"He said, 'I wouldn't have thought so.'"

We laughed.

"And he was a sweetheart, next to Stell. Stell outright scared me. I think she sensed it and would call me over to ask a question about a story or explain what was wrong with my lede. I loved when she did that, notwithstanding my fear of the Queen of the Desk Rats. It was a chance to learn. It was why I was there, really—not necessarily to become a real newspaper reporter, but to learn skills I could use in whatever became my so-called calling."

I just listened. It was a joy to hear the serious young fucker go on.

"I'd always thank Stell for the time she gave me, and sometimes she'd say I was worth it. Sometimes. One day, when I was feeling just a little of what Stell would call *my oats*, over a lede I'd written and she hadn't changed, I asked if she liked me just because I knew a subordinate from a dependent clause. Stell just smiled and said, 'They're the same thing, subordinate and dependent. Think about it. And I never said I liked you. I said you were worth the time. They *aren't* the same thing.'"

A knowing smile from your erstwhile reporter. "Stell used to say I needed to cut down on my auxiliary verbs," I said, "and my drinking."

We laughed.

"I must have won her over," James said, "the way I stood there taking it, enjoying it, even. I had this sincere need to learn. This deep want to be better—at everything, at life. I guess she saw it. So she became a sort of gruff grandmother to me, dispensing all manner of advice, about what to read—the Irish for short stories, she said, the English for novels, the Russians for doorstops—and what to do if you happened to encounter a woman with a better record collection than you."

"What was the advice?"

"She said, 'Don't mess around with a woman like that. Marry her.'"

"Ah, Stell. Long live the Queen of the Desk Rats."

"I never worked up the nerve to call her that. I just called her Miss Stell, and she called me Her Subordinate."

We laughed.

"I've told Tilly, my girlfriend, about her, about Tommy, about all of them. And I told her about you, Charley. I studied your stories—before they were edited and after. But there was hardly ever any difference. That's how I knew you were good. That and the details you found and placed, just so, throughout the story. As a sort of reward for the reader. Or a trail to follow. Clues. Crumbs. It was like a hike in the woods, reading your stories.

"I watched you work. I wanted to talk to you but something held me back. It wasn't that you were intimidating. You weren't. It's that you just seemed so deep in what you were doing. With your story. I told Tilly it was a little like you were in some trance, but happy. Blissful. So I never bothered you. I just watched. I liked to think I was learning, just by reading your stories, just by watching you work. That was enough.

"And then that one day, you sort of nodded at me."

"The bridge-jumper story," I said. "The touch you had on that one. Not just the detail and the tension of it, but there was a sort of understanding you seemed to have about the situation. Like you were inside the head of that poor man."

"No—not him. Her. The rookie cop who talked him down."

"Huh?"

"I think I saw the story—felt it; I mean really *felt* a story, for the first time—through her eyes. Being so young with everything ahead of her. That's how she seemed to talk him down. As if her own belief in the possible was enough for two people. Her incredulity that someone would close a book when there were chapters still to read, even though the man on the bridge was middle-aged and clearly troubled. He seemed a poor man in all ways. But she got to him, reached him. And I felt like I understood how."

"So Emily was right about that, too. Her winning streak continues."

"Emily?"

"My cousin, remember? She liked the story, too. Seemed to think you were seeing the story through the rookie cop's eyes, while I thought it was the poor man whose troubled head you were inside."

"Or maybe it was too good a story to mess up."

"Nah. I've seen reporters who would botch the rapture."

We laughed.

"Well, anyway. That's the day I came closest to feeling like I belonged, like I was a real reporter."

A hand on his shoulder.

"You did. You were. You belonged and you were the real thing. That's what breaks my heart about it."

"I'll be fine, Charley. Honest. I'm fine now, truth be told."

"So you can assure me you're not now nor have you been suicidal."

"Nah, just in love. You should try it, Charley."

"One thing at a time, Jimmy. I need a job first. You, too, I think."

"Oh, that's the other thing. I didn't want to tell you."

"Tell me what?"

"Tilly. She has a friend in an advertising firm downtown. She's gotten me an interview—I had it scheduled, actually, before they let us go. I'd already been thinking about it."

"Christ, Jimmy. You're going into advertising?"

"I don't know, Charley. I'm young. I want to do a lot of things before I'm old. This firm does a lot of creative stuff."

"I don't mean to judge. Well, I do, but. You know."

"I know. You care."

"I do, Jimmy."

"Anyway. Let's get together soon. Tilly and I, we could take you out to eat. We could go to her mom's restaurant. It's there on Cooper. It's great."

"One of those places with a name that's not a real word, with a chef who's a frustrated artist, where the patrons all secretly wish they'd gone to Cozy Corner instead?"

"Now, Charley."

"So, yes."

He just laughed and went on toward the little house. Just then, Tilly came to the door again, poked her head out.

"Coming, babe," he said.

"Hi, Jimmy's friend," she shouted at me. "Bye, Jimmy's friend."

She had a nice, warm voice, a quite fetching lilt.

"Nice to sort of meet you, Tilly," I shouted over my shoulder. "Take care of my friend Jimmy."

*

I stopped by the record store again on the way home. The clerk asked if I found Jimmy and I said I did. He asked if he was alive and well enough. I said he was.

"He's grand," I said. "He's in love."

"Yeah, Tilly. She's cool. She comes in, too. They met in here."

"What's she listen to?"

"Oh, all things, you know. Memphis soul to British sea shanties, anything and everything. You can't pin Tilly down. Anything up to yodels, pretty much. She's like her mom, that way."

"You know her mom, too? What's she like?"

"Kind of a bohemian, guess you'd say."

I think he just meant she'd reached middle age and still had good musical taste, but I said, "Christ, that's all we need in Midtown, isn't it? More bohemians and their *Look at me, look at me*. I suppose I could do it. I wonder does it pay? I don't have a job."

"What do you really want to do?"

"What I did."

I stood near the door, ready to go. I was looking at the little handbills they had posted on the wall. New bands were coming up every day. Some of them would last the week. There was one called Convent Nose Ring and another, called the Purr Kings, that apparently played surf-guitar versions of old Carl Perkins songs, "Dixie Fried" and "Blue Suede Shoes" and the rest. I didn't see one for the Church Keys. I wondered if young what's-his-name had found young-what's-her name. Had they reunited, or had he soldiered on alone, stepped out onto the edge of the stage, the cliff there, and sung his words to the drunkards down below? Had his girl made the coast and come to regret that tattoo, or was she the long-legged toast of Pascagoula?

The clerk said, "Really, Charley. What do you want to do?"

"I want to go home and put my feet up and have a bourbon."

"I meant for pay."

"Not much of that, sure," I said. "Oh, but the benefits …"

✳

I drove the little ways home. The help was off, or the help had quit—gotten word I'd been sacked and all. Or there was no help, had never been any help. That was it. It was just me, on my own and lonesome, like a verse in a song by Hank Williams, the Hillbilly Shakespeare. But I could fend. I could pour.

I made a bourbon, neat, and went outside to the front porch and set about to drink it. It's good to have a plan after you've had a long career at work you love and suddenly been sacked.

I sat back in one of the old, iron rockers and propped my feet on the railing. An old Coupe de Ville was parked across the street, had been there for months without moving. An orange cat jumped to the hood and crawled to the front of the thing and there stopped, then stretched, like a hood ornament grown fur. I thought maybe I'd do some heavy thinking but then I was saved from it when the phone rang.

"Flippen. How are you, man?"

"Aw, you know, Charley. I'm good when I drink and I'm good when I sleep. So far, so good."

"It's only been, what, three days?"

"That's what my wife says."

"She's right, I'm afraid."

"She's always right. I told her to bear with me a while yet. 'Bear with me'—I think those were actually part of our wedding vows. Anyway, I'll be fine, in time. Just no time real soon."

"Oh, hey, you know about James Ricketts?"

"Kid reporter? Screwing the daughter of the woman who has that new restaurant with the funny name in Cooper-Young, was already planning to go to the dark side—that ad agency—even before we got sacked? Yeah, what about him?"

"Never mind. He's fine."

"Well, what about you, Charley. How the fuck are you?"

"Oh, you know. Fucked. Doing poorly."

"Well, see, that's what I'm talking about. It's what I tell my Betts. You are fucked. You're supposed to be doing poorly. You're supposed to be drinking too much and moping around. You should have a drink in your hand right this minute."

I raised it and smiled. A fella walking across the street thought I was mocking him or something. He flipped me off with half his arm. Uncalled for!

"You should fight your friends' attempts to save you—for a while yet. A man who's falling needs a clear place to land. Your friends, they'll just have to understand. You'll come around. We all will. We'll have to, I suppose, at a certain point. My Betts will get sick of my moping. The dear woman's love will take the form of a cast-iron skillet."

Flippen broke himself up laughing. I joined in, a little. Then we said our goodbyes and I sat and drank and felt a little sad, thinking of young James Ricketts, who wasn't some Dickensian waif named for a childhood bone defect. He hadn't jumped from the Frisco or the Harahan bridge, either one, and they hadn't dragged the big river for his sad, soggy remains. He was young and in love with a young and lovely woman who had good taste in men, and in music. They were in a little, yellow shack of a house, having carnal relations to the likes of "Ride in the Chariot" and "Milky White Way." And I thought of Flippen, who drank too much but had a wife who loved him, who understood him, who could bear his drunkenness a while more yet, and then would come at him with a skillet, when it was time. Flippen, who married a woman with much patience, a good heart, and cast-iron wisdom. I thought about how I didn't have a woman who loved me enough to brain me like that.

I finished my bourbon and made one more. Bed, then.

For tomorrow, I would begin anew. Or, you know, the next day, whatever.

✳

That night I dreamed this: I was sitting on my porch, and black scavenger birds were pecking about me. There were three of the big sons of bitches. Crows, I supposed. One settled on my shoulders and looked down and in at my face. I wasn't dead but I couldn't move or speak. I was at his luncheon mercy. He moved close enough to peck out my eyes, but instead just peered in, then said, "Anybody at home in there?" He had a husky voice, for a bird. Another was nosing around my glass of bourbon. It buried its beak deep in the golden depths of the stuff, was down there a good, long while, and then came up came up saying, "Lordy, my." Like one of Old Man What's-His-Name's dippy birds, gone to seed. He had kind of a cartoon voice, high-pitched and loopy, but that may have been the hooch talking. The third of the birds was riffling through my wallet, to little avail. "Why, the bastard," he croaked. "Ain't a thing here but two dollars and a press card stamped *VOIDED*." That one had a voice I could almost place—he had some of my father's timbre and disgust.

The birds all at once looked up and at each other. They seemed to be communicating with their bird minds, as if human speech was fine for casual conversation, talking shit and what-not, but true discourse still required the ancient methods. They seemed about to turn on me, get down to some serious pecking.

Just then a man came walking up the walk. I thought he might have been in more of a hurry, given my plight, but I was glad to see the bastard, nonetheless. He waved his arms to shoo away the birds. "Shoo the fuck, now," he said to them. It was my friend Madison, the old columnist. He had an ex-wife with him. I couldn't remember her name. They seemed to have been out to dinner in Cooper-Young and were just on their way home. I wanted to ask him how the hell he was, but still I couldn't speak. I couldn't move or make a sound. The birds were as silent, suddenly. They had scattered to the far edges of the porch and there alighted to watch what might happen next.

"Is he dead?" the ex-wife said. She seemed more impatient than concerned, like maybe she sought to get amorous with her big, old ex-lug and maybe then they'd go and get married again. There was precedent.

"Charles, Charles. It's me, Madison." He shook me.

"He may only be sleeping," she said. "Which case, we should leave, Mad."

"You ever seen a real-live dead man, Lottie?"

Lottie—that was her name. Wife No. 2, if memory serves. No, wait—she's the one who married him twice. Only child of a professional gambler and a cigarette girl, Madison liked to say, raised rough but a real sweetheart. I never saw it.

"No, Mad, and I'd just as soon keep my streak alive. Let's scoot."

Ah, Lottie. Heart black as those birds.

Madison leaned in for a close look at me. I don't know what he saw, but I saw a man with a profound sadness about him. I wished to hell I could have talked. "Cheer up, Mad," I'd have said to my old friend. "Your life's work's been taken from you. But by all accounts it looks like you'll be getting some tonight." Was everybody getting some but me?

Now the birds flapped their big bird wings and made loud bird sounds. Madison and Lottie turned to see what the commotion was about. There was somewhat of a parade of my former newspaper cronies coming up the walk. There was Stell and Barboro and Flippen. Pearl, too, with a camera around his neck.

They all wanted to know if I was dead.

Madison said I was.

They looked at each other, as if they knew just what to do.

Flippen said he could write the obit.

Stell said she'd slap on a headline.

Pearl was already snapping pictures.

The journalistic necessities in hand, Barboro said he'd get the drinks.

And then they made a sort of party of it. They drank my beer and booze. They played my Junior Parker records. They told old newspaper stories—debaucherous tales that, alas, tended not to make it into the newspaper, city fathers with their pants about their ankles and the like. More people wandered by—there was Jimmy Ricketts and his lovely girlfriend, Tilly. There were perfect strangers, too, walking about the place drinking up my stock and listening to stories of dead me and saying things like, "He was a good man—Clarence, was it?"

I wanted to step outside my body, and go inside to bed. But still I could not move, speak. The scavenger birds, still silent on their porch perches, seemed to know this. They seemed to be waiting. But for what? They'd searched my wallet already. I was a good dollar shy of slim pickings, even.

"Here lies Charley Hull, a born newspaperman," Barboro said.

"The poor son of a bitch," Stell said.

Flippen poured fresh drinks all around and they lifted them to my memory. I wanted to say so many things. I wanted to say that two wakes in a week's time was a bit much for a man of my condition. I wanted to say thank you, and help, and could you do something with those birds, they make me a touch nervous.

Later, when the booze had given out and the freeloaders all gone home, and the last record played, and it was just old friends now, the night turned solemn, and serious things were said, warm and deep and heartfelt things, and then a welcome stranger did appear, as if by providence.

It was the young fellow we met at the wake, the fellow from the band, the Church Keys, the one whose girlfriend had run off to Pascagoula or wherever.

He stood just below the porch with his guitar, in the moonlight, and serenaded us all. He sang a spiritual and then he sang a lovely, little song we took to be one of his own. He had a clear, bright voice like a bell that rang out with those words of his, backing by the delicate chiming of his guitar. He finished the song and then said, "I only met Charley the once, so I don't claim to know his favorite song. But the night we met, he asked if I knew this one. So here goes ..."

Then he sang that dear favorite of mine, that old one by Stephen Foster.

"Hard times," the boy sang, "come again no more."

It sounded like a prayer, a plea, a requiem for the wreck of me. They all teared up at that—even the birds. Then they all let me be, dead me, walking slumping down the walk, leaning on one another for support, as much from the emotion as from my booze. Or they flapped away on broad, black wings, those that had them.

The ghost of me got up and turned in for the night. It slept deeply and liked to never wake up again.

3

# Future tense

Now began a bad stretch for your man. I was thrown out of two bars in Cooper-Young in one night. Or rather, as I was being thrown out of one, I shouted the name of my next stop. Tactical error. The bastards at the one called ahead, and the bastards at the other were waiting for me. I was foiled and accosted and told to go home before they had me arrested for being an asshole. I begged for a nightcap. It was a standoff, except they were standing and I seemed to have fallen in the shrubbery.

An old newspaper source of mine was coming out at the time and offered to drive me home. He was a developer, one time had the crazy-assed idea to turn the vacant Pyramid arena downtown into an indoor amusement park with rollercoasters, a Ferris wheel, and one of those spinny things where some eight-year-old boy invariably throws up on everybody. He let me out at my place.

I went inside to bed and rode the spinny thing all night.

✻

I holed up in the house. I rarely left. I wore little in the way of clothes. I swanned about in boxer shorts and a thrift-store bathrobe, red velvet with gold piping, that might have belonged, in a previous life, to some supper-club crooner or pro rasslin' queen. I slept one night in the tub and another on the kitchen floor. One morning, I got a look at myself in the mirror, and that was it. No more mirrors in the house! I put them out on the curb for the rag-and-bone man, good old Lauderdale Slim. Some mornings, I thought I ought to put myself out there.

✳

I grew a beard. (Wick said I looked like a homeless frontiersmen.)

I made a list of things I'd like to be. I painted them on the wall of my study, like Faulkner with his outline for that one book.

Recluse. Conjure man. Banjo player in a jug band.

Pied piper. Carny barker.

Charley the Revelator.

I wrote on the white walls in black paint. There was no one to tell me not to. There was no one to ignore me, even. The house was so haunted the ghosts had moved out—I wrote that sentence on a wall in the kitchen, along with other opening lines for novels I'd never write.

Guttersnipe. Codger. Ah, the possibilities abounded.

Second baseman. Second fiddle. Second Earl of Shaftesbury.

Third wheel. Tenth pin.

Homeless frontiersman.

William Faulkner.

(Emily said I was too old to be a guttersnipe and too young to be a codger, but the rest all seemed promising and I should pursue forthwith.)

✳

I drank a lot. I read more. I read daily from Steinbeck's *Sweet Thursday*, the sequel to *Cannery Row*. It might have been my favorite book of all time. Ah, Sweet Thursday—smack between Lousy Wednesday and Waiting Friday, our man Steinbeck said. I read from *Sweet Thursday* like it was the Book of Ecclesiastes.

✳

I came across a short story by Katherine Anne Porter, "That Tree," about a man who wanted to while away his life sitting in the shade writing poetry. His poetry was bad, but he didn't mind.

It wasn't about the quality of the poetry but the quantity of the shade. Alas, he ended up an "important" journalist, poor bastard.

✳

I was nearly thrown out of a bookstore on a Wednesday. This should not be possible. I was in the Southern Fiction aisle, intending to find something written in the last twenty years but inching as ever toward old editions of Faulkner and Welty and O'Connor I already owned. I overheard two women in the next aisle talking about memoirs they loved. I offered, through the stacks, that all memoirs were flaming shit-bags of lies and all memoirists should be lined up in the public square and … OK, well, yes, I may have suggested throwing lye in their faces. As a symbolic touch only.

I could hear one of the women scurry right off to the front desk to report the "disturbed person" in the Southern Fiction aisle. (Where else?) But the other woman seemed somewhat bemused, as if I might be a character in a book, slipped from the pages and come to life; a Snopes, say, or something out of Erskine Caldwell. Oh, to have been one of Flannery's peafowls, instead!

She said, "Memoirists don't claim to be writing the absolute truth of what happened. They're not journalists, of all things. It's honesty they're after. They're aiming a damn sight higher than mere truth, buddy boy."

"That's what fiction is for," I said. "That's why we have novels. For truth and honesty, both."

"Ha," she said. "Truth and honesty's not the domain of fiction writers—it's a leaping-off point. It's Cape Canaveral. Your fiction writers, they strap rockets and thrusters to truth and honesty, climb in, light the match, and blast themselves off to new lands and strange places, which they'll populate wholly with people of their own invention. They think they're gods, your fiction writers. Their novels are monuments to their own imaginations. If Faulkner had to limit himself to truth and honesty, why, the old crank would never have gotten out of bed in the morning. I love the man's work, but still."

This woman was formidable, quite possibly brilliant. I was unemployed and looked homeless. I pressed on.

"That's how you find truth and honesty," I said. "You go looking for it. You don't find it staring into the damned mirror, running your fingers over your precious scars, and then telling the story in a more interesting way than actually happened, with quotes so cutting and pithy they could only have been made up, after the fact, and then call the fucking thing a memoir—non-fiction!—because it's memoirs that sell these days, even though they're full of as much fiction as any novel, but without the integrity. Every memoir ought to come with a warning label."

"*Caution. This volume is a flaming shit-bag of lies.* Something like that?"

I said yes, and she laughed. It was dusky and sonorous, bit of torch queen in the lower register, and made me feel a little like a wind-up toy that talked—"Potty-Mouth Charley," batteries not included.

Just then the clerk appeared. He was a spindly, college-aged boy who looked like he'd been assembled that morning, and some parts of him were not yet dry. I thought I caught a whiff of carpenter's glue. He asked if there was trouble.

I said, "Yes. Thank goodness you're here. This woman is bad-mouthing fiction. Next she'll say the novel is dead. I'd like her hauled in on charges."

The clerk said, "Um, I meant you, sir. Are you being trouble? The other woman, she said you—"

"Disturbed, is it? Well, let me face my accuser. No, I don't need to. I can see her without seeing her. Wearing purple glasses and gypsy rags and got a 'Midtown is Memphis' bumper sticker slapped across her forehead. Which is about three inches too high, you ask me."

"Sir," the clerk began.

"Oh, he's all right," the woman in the next aisle said. "It's just his rocket ship doesn't go all the way up."

"Do you know him?"

"We've met."

"When?" This was me.

"Just now," she said.

The clerk shrugged and went back up front, then she whispered through the stacks: "The novel is dead."

A bit of hiss in her delivery.

I said, "Bah." It was the best I could do, against her superior intellect and sonorous tones.

She poked her head around the corner and said, "Bah to you." She was gone before I could see her face. I heard her laugh again, and then I heard the bells ringing on the front door as it opened and closed.

I thought I should chase her, ask her if she was doing anything Friday night, maybe we could go out and argue some more, or stay in and fight, whatever. Maybe I could borrow a couple, three gospel 45s from Jimmy, young friend, and see what developed. But I stood there, a wreck. I hadn't showered in days or shaved in weeks, and I was wearing that bathrobe over my clothes. Anyway, I probably couldn't have caught her, if she was lithe at all, me in my old-lady slippers from the thrift. (Hey, they matched the robe, as much as anything could.)

I spent another little while looking for something written in the last twenty years. Then I bought an old hardback copy of *Light in August* that someone had marked up in blue ink. One of the owners was at the desk now. She shook her head at me. We knew each other a little. She said, "Don't make me have to hire a bouncer, Charley. It's a bookstore."

"Oh, all right," I said like the scolded boy I was. "Sorry."

I called Wick to tell him what happened. "You're starting to engage with people. You're becoming the Charley Hull version of social," he said. "I've feared this."

"Fuck you, Elvis," I said.

✳

I repaired back home. I resumed imagining new careers and writing them on the wall.

Stunt man. Wing walker. Gandy dancer. (Ambitious undertakings, granted, for a man who recently fell in shrubbery while attempting to stand.)

Chimneysweep. Bootblack. Costermonger. Hasher. (Great, I could get a job as a character in a Dickens novel.)

Spirit. Specter. (The ghost of Hank Williams said I'd never get out of this world alive.)

Then it hit me. Bookstore bouncer!

∗

I drank the nights through. I slumped where I sat and slept where I fell. I sang songs of war, hard times, and heartache. Well, hummed. Then silence. Which I liked until it got so loud I had to turn up the music to drown it out.

I played the blues, mostly, the acoustic masters. Charley Patton and Skip James, Sleepy John Estes and the Mississippi Sheiks. Then I discovered electricity, and it was Elmore James and Howlin' Wolf, it was Little Junior Parker and His Blue Flames singing about how nobody do the boogie like the Blue Flames do.

I played so much blues the devil gave his two weeks' notice.

∗

I took long front-porch naps that fell somewhere between siesta and coma. Call me R.I.P. Van Winkle.

I read until the stories were real and the characters filled the house and I had to chase them out, for the sake of some peace. They were more troubled than me, poor souls. They cursed their authors and prayed to them, too.

∗

I had erotic dreams of a young Eudora Welty, her eyes dark as caves, daring me in.

Traveling salesman. Robber bridegroom. Petrified man.

※

Coffee. Reading. A hooty owl singing Hank Williams singing "Mind Your Own Business."

※

Another morning, a young man with a Holy Bible came up the walk while I was taking my morning coffee. I had been reading a lot of Flannery O'Connor those days. I'd left Eudora for Our Lady of the Peacocks. I'd just read that one story, "Good Country People," where the Bible salesman attempts to ply a young woman with liquor from inside his hollowed-out Bible. He later makes off with her prosthetic leg.

"Do you have a moment, sir?"

"Why sure, friend. Come on up here and let's have a righteous snort from that Bible!"

He backed slowly down the walk and scurried to safety.

※

Card shark. Confidence man. Moonshiner. Revenue man. Railbird. Barfly. Harpy. Dogsbody. Factotum.

Supper-club crooner. Pro rasslin' queen.

※

It rained and rained. For three days it rained. It came a storm. The lights blinked and flickered. I played Memphis Minnie's "When the Levee Breaks" seventy-two times in succession, setting a record of some sort.

Sand hog. River rat. Steamboat captain.

Flotsam. Jetsam.
Mike Fink and then some.

✳

Spring became summer. I spent it sitting on the porch and swigging from my jug of Old Severance, trying for the bottom, and claiming, if anyone asked (hardly anyone did, except Emily and Wick), to be thinking deeply of my future tense. I set deadlines and watched them pass—deadlines, once sacred to me, now held no sway. I wondered how they ever had. They were artificial things, pulled from the air and handed to me; I had accepted them like sacraments, pious fool that I was. I was Pavlov's dog, with opposable thumbs. But I don't remember ever getting any treats. There were never any treats. I had an editor one time whose idea of a compliment was, "It didn't suck too bad." It was the one heartfelt thing I ever heard the great horse's ass say, but he didn't even say that much to me.

Time passed in ticks, and then, in time, it made no sound at all. If fumes were a sound, that's how it sounded, like that, time passing. Time was something I smelled more than heard or saw—had a bit of a stench, like time had passed its own use-by date.

There was a bad tang in the air that summer. Or maybe that was me.

# Signs of life and poetry

One fall day, Emily came to see me. I was sitting on the porch with the newspaper. Ah, the morning rag. I was reading the obituaries, looking for the oldest of the freshly dead. On a good day, you'd find a few in their nineties, maybe one who pushed to a hundred. Imagine living that long. I couldn't imagine getting through the morning to lunch.

The obits, though, brought me comfort. The dead are better company—godspeed, Jewel and Buster and Rootie, Roosevelt and Quitman and Bertie. You can talk to the dead, or not; it's no matter to them. It's why I'd rather spend the day at Elmwood Cemetery than go to the Mid-South Fair.

"Ah, Buster," I said. "You were no Keaton, but you were a good Buster, still and all."

Emily took the last step up onto the porch, looked down at the sorry sight of me. She was seven months' pregnant now and even her usual glow had a glow; it had feathers, and an aura. Dawn and sundown would have bowed before her.

"Who the hell are you talking to, Charley?"

"The dead."

"Is it them I smell?"

"Now, Emily."

"Don't worry, I didn't come to badger you."

"Did you know that used to be a career—or a job, anyway. A badger was a fella who bought a farmer's goods and sold them at market. Peaches and beans and whatnot. A middle man, of sorts."

"Badger, huh, Charley?"

"I read that somewhere, yep. All part of my research on the subject of work, that toilsome pursuit. I could do that, badgering—except, you know, for the buying and selling part. That wouldn't suit me at all. And the travel, of course. All that to and fro. More of a homebody, these days."

"You should have been a homebody that night you got thrown out of two bars in Cooper-Young. Or the day you were damn near tossed out of the bookstore."

"You know about all that, do you?"

"You told Wick. Reported it, like it was news."

"Old habits."

"You need some new habits, Charley. And a damned job."

"Ah, my second act. You know what Fitzgerald said about second acts in America."

"Taking your cues from the Crack-Up, eh? He wrote a dashing sentence, but I wouldn't consider the man much of a mentor."

"Those dashing sentences didn't write themselves. They had to be lubricated."

"So are you writing, then, Charley? Or just lubricating?"

"Well, no. Not writing, per se. But I've been thinking about it. Ruminating. Call me Charley the Ruminator. I know that sounds rather like doing nothing at all, but I've got a lot to think about. Much cud to chew, as they say. It's about all I eat these days."

"Charley the Ruminator, huh? Or ruminant, I guess it would be."

"But enough about me," I said. "How's that budding nephew of mine? Is he a restless little bugger, I guess? Is he kicking like the dickens?"

"He is, that. He thinks it's how babies are born. They kick their way out."

"That's a good boy," I said. "You're lucky, Em. I envy you."

"It's not you who's got a fucking game of Kick the Can going on in his belly."

"But, ah, the gift of life. The miracle of birth. The wonder of it all. Would that I could, Em. Oh, would that I could."

"You, knocked up? Ha—you'd have to get laid first. How long's it been, Charley?"

"The mouth on you, Emily Carr."

She leaned swaybacked against the front-porch beam. She shook her head.

"That's about the only part of me that still works like it used to. I'd forgotten what it's like, in my middle age. I'm a damned cow, Charley. Bit of a ruminant, myself."

She pushed slowly away from the front-porch beam. She ached from the gift of life and the pending miracle of birth. The wonder of it all was a pain all over. She turned to go.

"You're a beautiful woman, all the more so for your condition. All the more so, and still more." I thought to say that bit about her glow's glow and her aura, those feathers. But I wasn't needing a smack in the chops, just then. I said, "Sit me with me, Emily."

"If I did, you'd need a crane to get me back up."

"Crane operator, hmm. That appeals. Me up there in the cab of the big beast, all alone at the controls, where they couldn't bother me. Pick up a little something and move it four feet to the left. How hard could it be? Like a little boy with his toys. Child's play on a somewhat larger scale. Crane operator, yep. I'll have to add that to my list."

"Your list, yes. Wick told me about the list. Most people use pen and paper."

"Faulkner wrote on his walls."

"So you've taken him for a mentor, too. How are they getting along, up there in your head, William and Scott?"

"Poorly, at best. Faulkner says he can't take seriously a writer who once wrote a story called 'Bernice Bobs Her Hair.' Fitzgerald says Faulkner wrote like he didn't want anybody to read it. Says you shouldn't settle down to a book of Faulkner with less than a stiff drink and a sharp machete. They go on like that. They'd throw bottles but for the blessed contents. But they do come together, in the end, over drinks and tales of their days as script whores in Hollywood. The lowest form of the art, Faulkner said, writing for the movies, and Fitzgerald said he'd drink to that. So he did. They did. I do."

"Sounds rather lively up there in your head, Charley."

"Oh, it is, Em. The Jazz Age comes to Yoknapatawpha County. Jay Gatsby, meet Flem Snopes."

"What would you write about, Charley. I mean, if you ever quit ruminating and actually write?"

I looked away before I said it.

"Us," I said. "That day in the woods."

*

We crossed open field until it gave way to thicket, and we crawled in, the brambles and thorns scratching dares on our pale skin. Free of the thicket, we came to a rise and climbed it. We crossed a clearing and down again—more brambles, more thorns, a thicker thicket—and then a river we could not name.

It was that summer. We spent it at our grandparents' place, down in the Delta. It was Emily, always dreaming up some damn fool thing for us to do, and me, a dog for the idea, tongue out, going along. It was the summer she shot me, or tried to—or anyway tried not to but couldn't not, quite. It was the summer of "pow," the summer of fate and portent, long legs, chase, and ache. The summer of our disconnect.

I was a young thirteen, and she was an old one. She was thirteen going on gin-soaked Memphis barroom queen, I heard my mother tell hers one time. I hadn't even said a cuss word. I wondered if cuss words kicked when you said them, like guns when you shot them. I could have asked Emily. She knew.

Then one day she took us to see the devil. Emily said he lived way out in the country. She said there were no roads or even paths to get there. She promised briars to crawl through and a river to swim, and a gorge—the only one in all the Mississippi Delta, she said, maybe the entire state—where we'd have to leap from one side to the other. She said it was forty feet across and two hundred down, but only three people had failed to make it, because no more had dared to try. She said if we made it that far, through the briars and across the river, and over the gorge, then it was just the devil, sitting on his porch with a Kentucky long rifle, and he'd play hell shooting both of us, if we came running at him from opposite directions. She said he'd probably just shoot the slower runner, so to go extra fast.

It was like having Daniel Boone for a thirteen-year-old girl cousin.

✳

She laughed at the memory. It was a lovely sight. The whole of her shook. Feathers flew.

Then she did sit down. It was like some kind of lunar landing—her words, not mine.

I went inside and came back out with a pitcher of ice water. I poured us each a glass.

✳

It was the summer my parents spent trying to save their divorce—the divorce they were threatening to get, anyway. That's how I heard my grandfather say it to my grandmother, as they sat on the porch, talking like they did over drinks at day's end. Hers was sweet tea and his was bourbon and water on the rocks, but sometimes they'd switch glasses, and she'd say, "So this is what it tastes like. I'd always wondered what the fuss was about," and he'd say, "You've been stealing my bourbon for going on forty years, and leaving me with this sweet tea to drink. You're lucky there's some history and children between us, or I'd have to put you out." She'd take one more sip and then hand the glass back to him. She'd say, "I've been put out for years. I just don't let on." They'd share a little laugh then, always, and then go on talking about their day, the state of the state of Mississippi, the Delta, and the wider world, or whatever family drama was playing out up the road in Memphis—usually involving their daughters, my mother and Emily's, and the awful men they'd married.

✳

"We were just kids playing, Charley. Trying best we could to amuse ourselves."

"I was a kid. You weren't," I said, and said no more for a moment, knowing she knew I was right.

✳

The river was twenty feet across. Emily called it a creek. She seemed disappointed there wasn't more to it. She was hoping for rapids fraught with danger and eighty-pound catfish, I guessed; maybe pirates, or the Great Armada of Arkansas.

"We have to cross it, Em?"

"Well, I guess we do, Charley," she said, "unless you think the devil, who wouldn't leave his front porch for God or a hurricane, is just going to come out here and meet us, and you could just shout your questions across the water and he'd shout back his answers. And then we'd say something like, 'Well, see you down the road, you devil, you,' and he'd smile and wave and we'd go on home, and Grandmother would wonder where we'd been, to get scratched up so, and she'd call Grandfather to come and see."

We both knew what he'd say. He'd say, "Why, they're just being boys and girls," as if anything up to trying to leap forty feet across the only gorge in the Mississippi Delta was laudable childhood behavior and should be encouraged. Then she'd say something like, "Why, I never," and he'd say, "Well, I did—twice, Sweets, just to make up for you." It was that gentle sparring, I think, that saw them through near fifty years of marriage; that, and the sharing of the family bourbon.

"Questions?" I said. "What questions?"

I was a yellow-haired, blue-eyed stalk of American boyhood, all bone and freckle, held together by wonder and doubt and questions that wanted no part of answers.

But Emily didn't hear. She'd unlaced her sneakers and thrown them onto the far banks and was already halfway across herself. I was still unlacing mine.

"C'mon, Charley. Hell. The water's not even up to anywhere indecent on me."

She really talked like that.

﹡

"You were quite the innocent, I will say," she said. "Thirteen and scared of life—of everything."

"Of you, most of all."

"But would do any damn thing I dreamed up."

"Yep."

"The hell I must have put you through."

"I'd have followed you to hell, if you'd have said the word."

"I'd have said it, if I thought we could get there on foot, from that nothing-doing little town."

"Ah—Slew, Mississippi."

"Saddest little town ever was. I think that's what the Welcome-to-Slew sign at the town limits actually said."

"It wasn't even the real devil who lived there, remember? You said the real devil lived up in Memphis, in a great mansion on East Parkway. You said this devil we were going to see was really just a lesser evil."

﹡

And it was the summer Emily's mother went away. No one in the family saw it coming. She didn't say much. She never said much; I heard our grandfather tell our grandmother one time that their daughters were just alike, except that one kept everything inside and let it stew and simmer, and the other preferred a full boil and the occasional kitchen fire. Our grandmother clucked at that and said, "God forbid either of them just cook something to a turn," and our grandfather said, "Well,

101

we never could tell either one of them a thing. I don't guess God would have better luck."

Emily's mother didn't let it out, even the summer she went away. She just left. She didn't even leave in any kind of a huff. She might have been going out for a dozen of eggs, except she was gone three months, during which she sent no word other than a weekly postcard to Emily saying she loved her. That was the one thing Emily said she knew already and didn't need to be told. The postcards came from places you could hardly find on a map—Respite, Arkansas, and Slope, Texas, and Legs, Arizona— and offered no clues as to her purpose or destination. She was heading west, was all the postcards told us; it was like she was beating her own path there. But she was back at the end of summer, in time to get Emily and her little brothers ready for school, still saying nothing much of anything. She and Emily's father stayed married, and poorly so.

So did my parents. I guessed that summer spent saving their divorce was a failure, or a success. I never could figure out which.

"Where do you think your mother is?" I asked Emily that day, on our way to see the devil. "You think she's doing all right?"

What I meant was, how do you think my parents are doing at saving their divorce, and what does that even mean? But I couldn't ask her, straight out like that. She'd have known. She'd have told me. And I was that yellow-haired, blue-eyed stalk of American boyhood, all bone and freckle, held together by wonder and doubt and questions that wanted no part of answers.

"I guess she's made California," Emily said. "I guess in a day or two I'll be getting a postcard from someplace called Elbow or Corn Flakes or Devil's Hind End."

She laughed then, for the first time on the subject of her mother's absence. It's like she decided, in that moment, that it would all be all right, that she would be—or more like, that she could cope and fend, whether it turned out all right or not.

I think that's where it began with me blurting out random words and phrases and places I'd never been or was like to go, because I shouted those words back to her: "Elbow! Corn Flakes!

102

Devil's Hind End!" And then I shouted the names of places I didn't know to exist, and people one might meet there, and other words as would have beyond my saying just seconds before.

"Gorge! Barn door! Three Finger!" I shouted. "Jawbone! West Onion! Blue mama!"

We broke out laughing, and then Emily took off running and I gave chase, all elbows and knees and wild hair trailing, about to come clean of our scalps. I couldn't catch her, but I don't know that I wanted to. I liked her out in front where I could see her, always.

(See: It wasn't that I was a boy in love with a girl I couldn't. It wasn't that, at all. I didn't even like girls yet, and, anyway, she hadn't decided she was one.)

✳

"Em?"
"What, Charley?"
"Nothing."
"Too much of nothing, huh, Charley?"
"Yeah, Em."

✳

We were sitting on a modest overhang of rock, our legs dangling just a couple, three feet above a creek bed. This, apparently, was the gorge. A long-legged girl could cross it in one good stride.

"My father, he has these—" She looked across that failed gorge, as if the word she was looking for was over there, like a clue or lost bauble. "Affairs."

I said the word, too.

"That's why she left, I think. Because she's tired of his affairs. He's a decent father—well, he's all right. He doesn't understand me but he tries, sometimes. And then sometimes he knows not to try. That's something. I wouldn't know what kind of husband

103

he is. I don't guess my mother gives him much idea of what kind of husband she wants or needs. But maybe if he didn't have those affairs. Or maybe if they didn't call them affairs. Then he might not want to have them. They sound like such grand things, don't they? *Affairs*."

I didn't think my father cheated on my mother. At least there was that. To the extent he required another soul in his life, he'd found the one he wanted. He'd found a woman who could take a punch and give it back in kind.

God help us. The human race, I mean.

*

I looked over at her pregnant self. It wouldn't be long now.

"Are you going to name him after me, Em?"

"Oh, of course," she said. "Well, you know, middle name. Elvis Charles Carr."

*

One minute passed, taking slightly more than its allotted time. An unseen crow mocked the minute and the seconds that made it so.

The crow cawed proverbs and river stages. The crow cawed sermons of doom. And I asked how much farther to the devil's place.

"Up over the rise and down again, Charley, if you dare," Emily sang out. "Up over the rise and down, Charley, if you do."

There was another thicket or the same thicket again. There were the same brambles, the same thorns, scratching something deeper than dares on our pale skin. We were crawling now, almost level to the ground, breathing the dust's fumes, tasting the dust's grit. We did as snakes do, and I wondered what our grandmother would say about that, what the crow would caw, and then Emily said, *shhh*, that it was just up ahead, over the rise.

There was no devil, of course—no lesser evil, even. There couldn't have been. To live up to what was in Emily's mind, he'd have been seven feet tall and carved from mountainside, with guns for hands and a live Arkansas panther on each side of him.

We came up over that rise and there was the back of our grandparents' place. She'd circled us the hell around and brought us home safe, if late for lunch. Our grandmother was on the porch, giving us the devil, for sure.

✳

We sat and drank the last of our ice water and said no more. We watched the street for signs of life and poetry. That old Coupe de Ville was still parked there. It hadn't moved in months. I wondered if the owner had died; maybe I could blame him for the neighborhood stench. Two boys on bikes tore by, one chasing the other. The first called the second a cocksucker and the second called the first a motherfucker. But they were just playing. It was like they'd just learned there was such a thing as cursing, and it was liberating to them, a way to misbehave with no apparent danger.

Finally, Emily said, "Are you anywhere near it, Charley?"

"Near what, Em?"

"The bottom."

"Oh. Pretty near it, I think."

"Will it hurt a lot when you hit it?"

"I think that's sort of the point."

"But then you check yourself for broken bones, right? And, seeing none, you pick yourself up."

"Dust myself off."

"And start again."

"Yes, go out in the world. Present myself anew."

"I'd shave first, I were you."

"Sharp machete!"

We laughed again.

Emily began the machinations required for a reverse lunar landing. I helped her up. We hugged, as well as we could. She said I smelled like a Superfund site. She said I needed ten showers, a swift kick in the arse, a paying job, and a good woman, in pretty much that order. I told her I didn't think it could happen in any other order.

*

Later. Along about sundown. The front lawn of the editor-in-chief's house, his old Colonial-looking thing in Chickasaw Gardens. Me, sober and clear-headed, shaved and otherwise shorn, scrubbed clean, even, and yet … pissing in the flowers out front.

# Humiliation, over easy

It was a bad idea, gone poorly from the start. I paid a boy walking by five dollars to go ring the doorbell and tell the man who answered that some damn fool was out pissing in his flowers. The boy said he couldn't say damn or pissing, either one, and I said he just did, and he said that was for demonstration purposes only. I offered him ten dollars, and he said for that he could say pissing but never damn. We settled on twenty, and I admired the kid getting paid by the word like that.

The editor-in-chief was tall and lean in what I guess you'd call an athletic way, with wispy, blondish hair that almost seemed green, in a certain light. His head was always tilted slightly to one side, the left, like a puzzled child or dog. But people seemed to take it that he was listening only to them. The man could wear a suit, I'll give him that. He looked like what he was—an educated fool, or an exceedingly handsome mannequin—and it served him well. He was glib on a limited scale and winning in a simple sort of way. His way with conflict was to deny its existence. He saw merit in every side of every matter brought before him, whether it was a newsroom fight to referee or local issue to editorialize over. He wished to leave no one unhappy, which ultimately had the effect of leaving no one satisfied. But you didn't realize it until later. You always walked out of his office feeling like you'd been treated to ice cream in one of those fucking sugar cones. He would have made a good president, by which I mean he would have made a shitty president. You know what I mean.

Now he opened an upstairs window. The boy ran. I called him a little yellow thing, and he said, "Fuck you, you damn fool with your dick in your hand." (Well, he had me there.)

So then it was just me, pissing in the flowers, and the editor-in-chief looking down from up there, like some idiot child king upon the local rabble. Somehow I'd imagined us more eye to eye, some piss splashing onto his imported loafers.

"Charley Hull—what's this?"

"I've spent months trying to figure out what I'd say to you, when I saw you. But in the end I keep coming back to this."

"This is it, Charley? Your grand statement?"

"It is," I said. "You don't seem to deserve any better. But I at least thought you'd come to the door."

"If I'd known—"

"Didn't seem wise to warn you."

"I understand why you're upset, Charley."

"You're an ineffectual twit, an empty suit. You always were. Some people liked you at the start but I never did. I knew straight away."

"You want to know why, right? Why you? Is that it?"

"I did. I do. Hell, I don't know anymore."

"What can I say?"

"God forbid the truth. You and the truth, never formally introduced."

"The business, Charley. It's dying."

"And you, peering out the upstairs window of your great Chickasaw Gardens manse."

"I'm under water, if you want to know the truth. Does that make you feel better?"

"A little," I said.

I finished pissing. Gave it a shake and back in my pants, like so. What the fuck now, Charley Hull, you sorry bastard?

"Lots of good, talented people were let go. We're long past trimming the fat."

"You still go to work every day, I guess. Still walk in with your sleeves rolled up, like there's some actual manual labor required in handing out ice cream cones like you're the Good Humor man. Hell, you are the Good Humor man! It's the secret to your success. It's how you rose to such a lofty position, to live in such a grand house, to marry that wife of yours. Faith, is it? Hope?"

"Effie."

"I never liked her—her type."

"What type is that, Charley?"

"Thinks she's oh-so-original, special, interesting in all she does and thinks and says. The way she flits about."

"You're talking about the love of my life here, Charley."

"She thinks her cats purr in Italian."

He straightened his head—his version of a dog trick, I guessed—and smiled down at me. It was that smile he brought out for every newsroom dispute. No one ever was punished, under his watch. Plagiarism, fabrication, ethical lapses, outright incompetence—no matter. I heard one newsroom type say you could walk into his office, piss your name into the deep pile of his carpet, and not even get suspended.

Then, when the business began to die, came the layoffs. So he presided over our decline in the one damn fool way he knew. Maybe that's why they'd given him the job. Because he was perfect for it, in their minds. Management, I mean. Ownership. He even smiled to those he let go. He smiled to them most of all. They got chocolate sprinkles on their ice cream. I asked did it come bourbon-flavored, the day he let me go. He just looked at me confused, but smiling, still.

"She's left me," he said now.

"Your wife, Faith? Hope? Not Chastity, from what I heard."

"Effie."

(That was low, Charley, even for you.)

"So you were riffed, too."

(Lower still, C.)

Yet he was smiling. How did he do it?

"Will you have a drink with me, Charley?"

Well, Jesus Christ impaled on a copy spike at deadline. Had it come to this? I was now to sit with the man who'd fired me from the only job I've ever loved or wanted? I'd watered his flowers and now we were to share a bottle of Old Pity?

"It's not like I've got work to go to," I said.

✳

One drink, two.

"I wasn't as bad as all that, was I, Charley?"

We were sitting on the wraparound porch, under hanging gardens and a couple of ceiling fans, drinking his best bourbon. The light was hitting that wispy, blondish hair of his so that it did look green, or anyway greenish. They said when they sent him to us that he was sage. I guessed all along they were talking about his hair.

"You were bad enough," I said.

From somewhere came the sound of classical music; maybe his wife's cats were inside with cellos and double bass.

"As bad as my predecessors, in your eyes?"

He was three drinks in and getting maudlin. I was likewise but still feisty.

"Ah, don't get me started on the lot of them. Tinpots and tosspots. Self-styled intellectuals, ineffectual twits. Some were just bullies, was all. A few meant well, I suppose—you had to watch them most of all."

"You're just listing random bosses you've had throughout life, aren't you, Charley?"

"So?"

"What about me?"

"You're just fishing for insults now."

"Well?"

"You were as bad but in a different way. That's how it went with editors, sometimes. The next one would be a reaction to the last one—it was ownership's way of admitting its blunder, covering it up with a brand-new but different one. That's how we ended up with an ice cream man. It's a wonder they didn't give you a funny little white hat to wear and a bell to ring."

"People like ice cream, Charley."

"They do."

"So I gave it to them. It's a wonder how well it works."

"Sometimes."

"Quite often. Usually."

"It's not a cure for fabrication."

"No, that's true."

"You know what it tells a whole newsroom of reporters when you let shit like that slide?"

"I didn't let it slide, per se."

"Per se."

"What would you have had me do, Charley? Have him shot on the loading docks at dawn? Hand him over so you all, the newsroom mob, could string him up?"

"You think we wouldn't have?"

"That's exactly what I thought you'd have done."

There was a reporter, I won't even repeat his name, who invented a South Memphis drug lord. Fascinating fellow, this drug lord—quoted Cesar Chavez, played blues guitar like Albert King, and was thinking of going legit, maybe even running for mayor. Not that such a person couldn't exist, in Memphis, but this one didn't. The reporter made him up, whole-clothed the fucker. He spent months on the project, doing nothing else. He committed the greatest of all sins in our so-called calling. It didn't make the paper but came entirely too close. Enough people in the newsroom started casting doubt and outright calling bullshit that the editor-in-chief had to summon the reporter to say what should always go without saying: that every word he'd written was true. The office door was closed for a very long time. Then the story was quietly pulled—as quietly as anything ever happens in a newsroom.

"You don't know what was said, Charley."

"I know what wasn't—'You're fucking fired, you fucker, from here and every other newspaper in the fucking country, when I get fucking done spreading the fucking word on you, fucker.'"

"It's not that simple. It rarely ever is. You can't just call people fuckers."

"Fucker," I said, but with less edge than I'd intended.

He poured us two more. The cats were working on a Bach suite. They weren't half-bad.

"He admitted it, right?"

"He admitted to other things, too, in other stories. Small things, meaningless things, really, but, well ..."

"I see. Christ. So it would have been too great an embarrassment. So he had you—had a bargaining chip. Bring you down with him. You, who had been his personal editor on the project. You, who championed the work. He could have ruined you, too."

"It wasn't about me."

"Per se."

"It was about the paper. All of us. The institution. Journalism, really."

"You're making a pretty good case for having handed him over to the newsroom mob."

"He worked on major investigations for years. There were awards—Green Eyeshades and others. The series on the church burnings—remember that? It was a Pulitzer finalist. Should have won. But it was more than that. Stories he worked on, they resulted in legislation, resignations, jail time. He did great work until he didn't."

"So for the good of the newspaper he was allowed to retire, and for anyone reading between the lines he'd had a sort of breakdown. The stress of the work."

"It wasn't only my decision. Lots of things weren't only my decision."

"Why'd he do it? Did he say? Did you even fucking ask?"

"He said he got bored."

"So do I, sometimes. It's why there's bourbon and the arts."

"And, he said it became a bit of a game."

"There are things for that, too," I said. "Poker. Checkers. That one where you try to conquer the world with dice and little, tiny soldiers."

"Anyway, it was a proper cockup, and I made of it what I could. He quietly, as you say, retired. Fortunately, it hadn't made the paper. If we hadn't pulled it, God knows what we'd have done—had to do."

"Straight to bed with no ice cream?"

"You have a child's view of the business, Charley."

"In my view, it's not a business."

"You sitting here, bitter and unemployed, is proof otherwise. It's a business and we make business decisions and sometimes they're not ones we're entirely proud of. But it's more at stake than pride. So we let him retire. Quietly. Or at least as quietly as anything ever happens in a newsroom."

"Did you sleep that night?"

"No," he said, wearily, "but the next night I did. It's the thing about being the editor, a thing you have to learn. The newspaper's black and white. Life's not."

"I'd like to have been editor-in-chief for about fifteen minutes."

"That's about how long you'd have lasted, Charley. God love you, but it's so."

"You're saying we're no better than any other institution that's built and wired to protect itself, the institution, at all times, above all, at whatever cost."

"That's exactly what I'm saying, Charley. I'm not sure I could have, would have, said it sober. But there you go."

"You're saying ethics are more, what, a hobby?"

"I wouldn't say that, no. They're sacred. They are. It's a mortal sin to break them. But we sin sometimes, and sometimes mortally."

"No better than the government, then?"

"Pot 'n' kettle, sometimes, I fear," he said. "And anyway, remember, the story got pulled. Killed. The system worked."

"Barely. And thanks mostly to the newsroom mob."

We didn't talk for the next bit. We drank. We looked out from under the hanging gardens onto his vast lawn. He gave a wave at it all, as if to say—I don't know. I don't think he did, either.

"So tell me, Charley," he finally said. "Now that you know a little more. Was I as bad as all that?"

"As bad as the worst of them?"

"Yes. I guess."

"Well, I never drank bourbon with the others."

"My predecessor, whose name you probably don't want to hear, he's old and sick and dying, you know. He's in that big house in Overton Park. He's alone."

"Well, there's that."

"Will you go to his funeral?"

"It'll be me starting the fucking wave." But now I sounded maudlin.

"Charley, Charley," he chided.

"It's just editors I'm bitter about." I sensed a slight rally. "And publishers, of course. They were worse. Don't get me started on the likes of them. Princes of fucking darkness."

"Well, sure, publishers," he said. Because even bosses have bosses.

We laughed.

Then we fell back to silence, to drinking. Dusk had left us. Dark appeared, walking woozily up the walk. I stood to go, a little woozy, myself. No condition to drive. He said I could sleep it off inside but I said no, I don't like cats.

"It's just the dogs and me," he said. "She took the cats, Charley."

I said, well, it's like that one song by Joni Mitchell. But I forgot which Joni song it was. He said he thought he knew the one. I don't know how he could have.

I slept the night in the porch swing. I woke up to the sound of the newspaper hitting the porch. The old familiar *whap* of words on stone. *Fucking fuck me, fucker.*

Somewhere a bird sang and then another. It was a cool, fall morn. You could call it crisp and not be far wrong. I didn't even have a hangover. Speaks to the quality of the bourbon, perhaps. (Mental note to self: Buy better hooch. Also, get a job.) The editor-in-chief was in the kitchen; I heard the hiss and crackle of eggs and bacon, smelled coffee. And soon I'd feel some dog's cold nose on mine.

I'd hit bottom and landed in feathers and down. I'd accepted comfort and aid from the enemy.

A new low for your man, his humiliation complete, over easy.

4

# Tales of ancient grease

### EX-SCRIBE FINDS WORK, SUCH AS IT IS

The jukebox repairman took the back from an old Wurlitzer and looked inside. He crouched before it. He rocked back on his heels and then from side to side. He might well have been looking inside his own head. That's how it seemed, watching him work.

It was winter. I'd gotten a sort of job. Proud of me? Don't be. I was the jukebox repairman's apprentice. Or I was a reporter without a story to write, I don't know. I wasn't making any money but it got me out of the house, gave me somewhat of a purpose, a place to be. Really, it allowed me to hang out in bars and muse on old records with a fellow lost soul.

He peered inside the old thing. There were cobwebs. There were wires of varying thickness and various colors, some frayed and wrapped in electrical tape; some of the tape had gone brittle and begun to crack. There were springs and bolts and screws, gunked in gray-black matter for which science surely had no more scientific name than gunk. There was ancient grease that all but gleamed.

I'd known him a bit—wrote a story about him, years ago, back when repairing jukeboxes was a thing some people still did. Then I ran into him again, in that pirate-themed dive bar on Broad. I asked if I could tag along as he worked. His name was Donnie Ferriday—Ferriday, like the town in Louisiana where Jerry Lee Lewis was from. He seemed as wrecked as I was. I liked him. It was fate that we joined up, I wanted to think.

"Look here," he said.

I leaned in.

"Where?" I said. "At what?"

But then I knew. I could see it.

There were dim tubes all in a row, the dimness seeming like a swaying presence, small ghosts, a choir of them about to take up some solemn hymn of healing. There was a belt that sagged. There was a single tiny bulb, its delicate guts like something about to flutter to life, fly away and seek some spring flower on which to alight. There were three speakers, and an amp, flecked with rust, in which he could almost see his reflection. And I, my recent past.

Ah, reporting. I hated the part where I actually had to talk to people. I had to force myself, because without it you had no story, or only a shell of one. But the part where I could shut up and watch, take down every little detail, hoard the little bastards for later use—I loved that part. I loved it almost as much as the writing.

"Can you fix it?" I said, stepping back to give him room to work. But he just leaned back in.

The jukebox was an early Sixties model, a steel monstrosity, not one of the pretty ones from a few years before. But it had its charm. It was like a big, old funky washing machine or something.

It was as if he really could see his reflection in there—rust flecks like the red freckles of his feckless youth. He'd told me he grew up "normal, whatever that means," in a small town in Kentucky, with parents who loved him, a brother who didn't, two sisters who never noticed him one way or the other. He played ball, grew tall, did boy things, discovered music and girls, and one of them loved him back, always and forever.

"I was bright with my hands," he said, meaning he understood how things worked, why they didn't, without his head ever being the wiser. He could fix anything, tune two forks and a butter knife into a short-wave radio, pull in D.C. taxi cab dispatch, Tex-Mex dance bands. His mind couldn't explain what his hands were doing; it was as if, he said, his mind wasn't privy. He said the better his hands got, the more his brain seemed to recede. He became damned near inarticulate—or anyway, an introvert's introvert. I told him I understood. I did. The only difference was, I lived in my head, all my skills there, taking in all the tiny details I saw, turning them into newspaper stories. Not that I could talk much of a game, or do with my hands the one thing my profession asked for but fortunately did not require of me—to touch type. I was a two-finger banger of the keys. The both of us, stunted, you'd have to say. Made halfway, parts missing, set aside. So we understood each other perfectly ...

I leaned back in now, but not so much that I crowded him. Craftsman at work.

It really was his own reflection he was seeing. I was convinced. Because suddenly he looked away. His eyes poked elsewhere, for a diversion: levers, clamps, fuses, switches, bolts, tubing, black-lettered cryptic edicts in all-caps about red jumper plugs—"What the hell's a red jumper plug and why the all-caps edicts?" I said, but he didn't say—and finally, yes, the songs, the music, the wondrous sounds inside the thing. Those great old scratchy records, like those inside his head. Mean Chicago blues that would cut you where you stood for the dime in your pocket. Memphis guitar instrumentals so filthy-sounding the radio wouldn't play them, even without words. Country weepers out of Nashville. High slink up from New Orleans. And a thousand young British snots, shouting America's music back to it over the barb and squall of a thousand cheap guitars. Some love songs, even, I supposed; some people still had need or want or use for those. He rocked back again on his heels, seeming to listen to them all, all at once, a medley in his head.

MEMPHIS BAR TO CLOSE; FIRST TIME FOR EVERYTHING

"So can you fix it?"

It was the old man who owned the bar. It was a dive in Midtown, not far from Overton Square. It was going out of business. It was in a rundown little building that had been

118

bought for the land. The land would become a parking lot for the place next door, a restaurant with a name that wasn't a real word, where they were doing interesting things, I'd been told, with figs.

Still the jukebox repairman said not a word. He stuck his whole head in the thing. I half expected his body to follow, like it was a machine for time travel, and he'd find himself, after some poofs and minor explosions and lots of smoke, sitting front row watching Howlin' Wolf and his band bring down some little juke in Bar Brawl, Arkansas, in 1952.

After a minute or so, he pulled his head out, turned, and looked up blankly at us. Then he went back in. I just shrugged.

My name is Charley Hull, and I am the unpaid apprentice to a time-machine repairman in the lost city of Memphis, Tennessee.


EX-SCRIBE WALLOWS YET SOME MORE; TO THE CARRS A BABY BORN


"So can you fix it?" the old man said again.

He'd come out from behind the bar, a rag in one hand and a highball glass in the other. He walked with a waddle and stood with a stoop. He stood behind the jukebox repairman, seeming to try to read his body language, divine it for defeat.

Finally, Donnie spoke, if you'd call it that.

"Well," he said.

"Well's no good to me, son," the old man said. His landlord had begun this same way, he said. "Give it to me straight."

Donnie did not turn or speak. He scooted back on his haunches for a broader look. Slump-shouldered and listing, he looked at the old machine as if he had been hired to make it rise from the floor and play "Elevate Me Mama" by Muddy Waters.

I moved up alongside him. I felt for the first time the cool dankness of the drafty old barroom. It was February, when even Memphis gets cold. I'd done some freelance writing to pay the bills, what bills there were. I was living simply, eating soup and drinking cheaper and cheaper hooch; it was tin cans and plastic bottles for your man. Seems like I'd achieved my only other childhood career dream. I was a hobo, but a half-assed one, at that. I didn't hit the open road. But at least I was getting out of the house a little. Donnie came by in the mornings, on days he had a job. It was only about once a week, and some weeks not at all. I'd sold my car in December and bought a clunker, and with the difference had rent for a few months. (It's not all as romantic as it sounds, dear reader.)

Oh, and I was an uncle again. Emily had a little boy who wailed like a tenor sax. She said she was too old to raise a young 'un but he was such a handsome little pup, with such stout lungs, that she thought she'd keep him. Wick grinned like he might be the pup's slightly older brother. I said he'd grow up, in Wick fashion, to inherit the consultancy, sell the thing, and open a cigar stand. He was a fine lad, but oh, that wail. He could have opened for Little Junior Parker and His Blue Flames at Club Paradise. His name was Jesse C. Carr. Emily said they'd tell me what the "C" stood for once I got proper work. Apprentice to the jukebox repairman did not, in my dear cousin's eyes, constitute such.

## GOOD GREASE HAILED AS HEAVEN FOR HINGES

It had been a long winter, but now winter was like an old man with a limp and a shuffle, just trying to get out of its own way. Donnie said he felt like an old man himself, though he was barely fifty. He complained of his aches—lower back when he stood for more than a few minutes, knees after he crouched for any length of time. Mostly, he said, he felt old up inside his head. He felt old the way the jukebox, with the back off, looked old— old wires, old springs, a sagging belt, dim tubes. That gunk. He stood, though, without too terribly much strain.

"Good grease on the hinges, must be," he said.

He smiled at this thought, and at the song, I guessed, up inside his head. I tried to listen and imagined I could hear it. A

Chicago blues shout gave way to a Memphis soul strut and then to New Orleans second-line pomp.

He said to the old man without turning his gaze from the Wurlitzer, "I'm a '63 model, myself."

## SAD MEN COMMISERATE OVER BOOZE, SADNESS

Donnie and I sat at the bar, drinking coffee, and the old man stood behind it, washing highball and pint and shot glasses, and then setting them on the nubbed rubber mat to dry.

The silence in the place was far too noisy and suited none of us—the creak of the plank-wood floor as the old man shifted his weight while he washed the glasses, the metal wheeze of the barstool as we leaned forward to sip our coffee. The low hum of refrigeration and the resigned sigh of the heating unit seemed to be speaking to one another; there seemed to be the makings of some truce between them. There was the blink and flicker of the lights overhead and busy fritz of neon in the front window. There might have been a cricket, somewhere in the crevices of the old joint, shivering and covering its ears.

"Can I get you something for that coffee?"

Donnie said he wasn't much of a drinker. He said when kids his age were discovering drink, he was holed up in his bedroom, listening to records. He said his first love had been an old Etta James album cover, the *Rocks the House* LP, from his father's collection. He said it was like finding some nudie mag in his old man's closet. Then he heard the thing. I remember hearing it, too. My, my, Miss Etta.

The old man just shook his head and smiled like he somehow knew, or knew the type. Hell, he knew all types. He was a bartender. We were sort of kindred spirits that way. He looked at me. He knew my type, too—parched.

I said I drank too much, but never during work hours. He looked mock askance at me.

"I'm the jukebox repairman's apprentice," I said.

Donnie shrugged.

"What," the old man said to me, "could you not get hired on with the stagecoach?"

I raised a coffee mug to the old cuss. He poured himself a shot from a bottle and raised it to us. He drank the shot and then washed the shot glass. He set it on the nubbed rubber mat to dry. He said without looking up, "Not to be a stuck record about it or anything, but can it be saved?"

"The jukebox?"

"You're the jukebox repairman. I reckon the jukebox."

"Well—" Donnie paused and then stopped. He stared but not at the old man; he seemed in need of some itch to scratch.

"Man walks into a bar, says to the bartender, 'Give it to me straight.' It's like that. Just tell me. It's just a jukebox."

*Just?* None of us believed it.

"I can fix it—"

"Good man."

"—but it'll take a week and might work for a day. I don't see the point."

"I take it you don't put that on your business card."

Donnie looked at the old man as if to say, *Business card? This is no business. This was a folly that cost me my wife and son. Who quits perfectly dull office work with perfectly middling pay and benefits to repair jukeboxes? Nobody gets anything repaired anymore. They just buy new. And nobody plays these little 45s I stay up dreaming about, still, like I'm stuck at sixteen. That's it. That's me—a stuck record.*

That summed up Donnie's story, as he'd told it to me, slowly, over the weeks. The old man seemed to have suspected as much. He tried to cheer Donnie, in his way. He reminded him the bar was closing for good, that it would be demolished to make way for nothing, for an asphalt parking lot for that restaurant next door.

"So why fix the jukebox?" I knew the answer, but I thought it would do us good to hear it.

"Because I ain't dead yet."

## STUFF SMITH FIDDLES WHILE YOUNG BOY LEARNS

So there we were, a flock or wreck or whatever you call a gathering of poor bastards. Even the bar had grown silent. A song would have been nice, for to bring us up out of the funk we were in, but, you know, broken jukebox and all. Donnie, in particular, was in need of some uplift. The old man tried again.

"Your name's Danny, right?"

"Donnie."

"All righty. Donnie, it is. Mine's Archie. So tell me, what's your favorite song?"

"My favorite song? Hell, I don't know."

"Sure you do. I saw the way you looked at the jukebox. I've seen men look at women that way. I used to look at my ex-wife Queenie that way."

"OK, what the hell. It's an old one."

"I'm an old man. Try me."

"'When I Grow Too Old to Dream,' he said. "I guess it's a standard. It must be, by now. It's been done by everybody, by Louis Armstrong and Benny Goodman, the Everly Brothers. But I mean the version by the Nat King Cole Trio."

"I know that one."

"But it's not because of how Nat King Cole sings it. He's fine and all. But it's his violin player, you know."

The old bartender nodded. He seemed to know a story was coming; men adrift, men lost, men whose lives stuttered like a stuck record, they always liked to tell stories about how they got that way, where it all began, those small moments on which a life can pivot or slip. I nodded, too.

"We had this old man in my little hometown, up in Kentucky," he began. "Homeless, I guess you'd call him. But I don't think we ever thought of him that way—you know, thought of him as having no home—though I couldn't have told you where he lived or for sure that he lived anywhere. Kids don't think about those things.

"He wore this little, old pork pie hat and stood on a corner of downtown, what downtown we had. My father had a store, he sold appliances. TVs and record players. He sold records, too. He'd let me act like I was working there, when I was a kid. I'd play a record on one of those record players and act like I was demonstrating it to some imaginary customer. Then one day I got bored with the imaginary ones and called in the old man. We called him Scary Joe, all us kids. But he wasn't, really. Scary, I mean. He looked sad, more than anything. So I just called him Joe. That day I did. I called in ol' Joe and tried to sell him a record."

The old man, Archie, poured himself another shot but didn't drink it. He leaned against the back of the bar and listened, head cocked upward, as if to some old tune.

"So I played that record and stood back. I crossed my arms, like I'd seen my father's salesmen do. I sort of leaned backward, like there were imaginary dancers that had sprung up from the old tile floor of my father's store and I wanted a better look. I may have closed my eyes and seen them.

"Well, Scary Joe stood listening. I guessed he was listening. He was looking at the old tile floor, like he saw the dancers, too, but didn't have the nerve to look at anything but their feet. He always looked down, no matter. He'd never look you in the eye. You'd see the front brim of that pork pie hat and then you'd see the folds of his rumpled face. But then I looked and saw his foot sort of tapping in those old shoes of his."

Donnie smiled, just slightly, as if a smile were something to ration over the course of a long day in a life somehow both stuck and adrift. He said, "Well, the song ended and I said, 'What do you think of that, Joe?'"

Donnie leaned forward as Archie poured him another cup of coffee.

"Scary Joe, he said, 'Stuff Smith.' I just looked at him. I'd never heard him talk before then. None of us kids ever had. He was Scary Joe. He was a pork pie hat and folds for a face and chin stubble. He was a sad ol' drunk—drunk's what people called him, what they said he was—even though I never saw him so much as sip anything. The story was that he was young once, and some said brilliant, or anyway book smart, and had a wife, and some said she was beautiful and others plain but from a rich family, and that he lost it all, and his job, too, whatever that was, because of his drinking. But I thought, even then, that it was just a story the old generation told the young one to keep us from drinking. Anyway, I'd never heard him talk before. He didn't talk much, by the sound of him. He seemed out of practice. It was a hell of a voice, the damnedest-sounding thing. It sounded like an out-of-tune toot from some old horn.

"'Stuff Smith,' he said again, and I looked at the album cover, and said, 'No, Joe, it says here that's Nat King Cole,' and he just said, 'Stuff Smith.' It was like those were the only two words he could say, the only tune he could play on that old horn. I was wondering if that was his name, that Scary Joe was really somebody named Stuff Smith. I don't think I'd ever considered that he had a real name—that he was anything other than what we kids called him.

"Well, about this time my father came and sent me to the stock room to go and get a box of nothing. He gave me a look— you know, that look fathers give. He shooed Joe to the street corner outside. There were real customers, proper men and women, with money to spend."

Donnie shook his head, broke into a grin; it happened before he could think to ration it out.

"It was only later, you know, when I came to realize it. I looked at the album credits. Stuff Smith was the violin player. Hell, he was the one who made the song so great. It was him, even if nobody much knew it but some old man who people called scary and drunk but wasn't either one, I don't guess, looking back."

The old man poured a second shot and a third. He handed them to us. He said we were off duty now. We clinked glass and Donnie paused, but only to ask, "What are we drinking to?"

"To looking back," Archie said.

I drank mine anyway.

## MEN IN BAR MUSE ON LIFE, LOSS, THAT ONE SONG BY JOE TEX

There was another shot and then another—well, for the old man and me. Donnie was still nursing his first. He looked at it like the '27 flood was in there. But then he knocked it back, good man, and another. Then Archie poured us tall whiskeys with water to slow the pace. We began to talk, the three of us, about everything and nothing, about B-sides to beloved records and obscure session musicians, about the history of the bar and the time that it became, briefly, a gangster's hideaway. Archie talked of Queenie, his ex-wife, and said she would have been a good gangster's moll. "Skinny legs and all," he said, "Skinny legs and all." Donnie said, "That was a good song, that one," and Archie said, "James Brown?—no, no. It was Joe Tex." And I said, "They had a feud, Joe Tex and James Brown. I think James actually took a pistol shot at Joe." Donnie said, "I think it was over a woman, the wife of the one or the other." It was almost wistful, the way he said that last part.

Archie spoke of feuds and fist fights and outright brawls, a sort-of greatest hits of the old place. Then he stopped himself, and said, apropos of whiskey and regret, old age and the impending death of his bar, that he missed and still loved his Queenie. "Hook nose and all," he said. "Hook nose and all." Donnie said, "Did she leave you for another man?" and Archie said, "Nope, just left. I was here. I was always here. That was the thing. She said she was my wife but this bar was my mistress, and so this place got my best, what best I had. I said, 'It's not like that, Queenie'—like men say, you know, when it's exactly like that."

Donnie said, "Mine said—well, she said, 'I'm not leaving you for another man, Donnie, but I fully intend to find one.' She did, too. He's a good man, I have to say. He has a perfectly respectable office job and all that. They moved to Missouri, a perfectly respectable little town there, in the Bootheel."

Archie asked if he loved her still, if he missed her, and Donnie said, "I don't know, honestly. I think the both of us chose poorly. We were never really happy together, or right together. But I damned sure do regret what I did to her, and to our son. My damned dream—my damned fool notion. Jukebox repairman! Am I the biggest fool ever come down the pike?"

He seemed pretty well soused now. It hadn't taken much. He paused as if there was no more to say, ever. But then he said, "I am sorry, I truly am. But no, I don't still love her. I'm not sure I ever did. Honest to God? I'm not sure I ever fully got over that Etta James album cover. Etta, she sort of ruined me for other women, I think."

"What about you, Charley?" Archie said. "Did you never marry?"

"I almost did, once."

"You want to talk about it?"

"You ever, in all your days of bartending, Archie, have anybody answer yes to that?"

"They always say no, then they start in talking. It's a dirty trick, I know."

"I wasn't above using it, myself. I think the trick was invented by reporters. But there's not a whole hell of a lot to tell. I met her working on a story—it's the only way I ever met anybody. This was years ago. The story was about a kidnapping, a girl, teenager from a rich family in Germantown. She'd been one of the girl's teachers. I interviewed her. We talked a lot. Well, she talked, I listened. The girl turned up—she'd orchestrated the whole thing. It was all over in a few days. But the woman, the teacher. We kept talking, after the girl had come home and the story was over. It was like before. She talked, I listened. I didn't mind it. She had a lovely voice, like song, almost. I think she was desperate to get married, was the thing."

"What about you?"

"I was willing."

"The desperate and the willing."

"That was us."

"So what happened?"

"She had this crazy idea, only it wasn't so crazy. It was smart. She said we should take the honeymoon first, just to see how we got on as married folk. So we started planning the trip, you know. She wanted to go on a Caribbean cruise. I said fine, sure, whatever. But she said we had to decide together. Partners for life and all. So she asked where I'd really like to go. Ireland, I said. She wanted to be out in the sun and I wanted to be in some dark pub. That got us laughing about how different we were, and then it got us *thinking* about how different we were. Well, you know how it is—all of the sudden we were *talking*, having an actual conversation, about how different we were. We couldn't agree on a single damned thing. Not books or movies or food or religion or politics. There was no end to it. She liked cats, wine, show tunes. And me, you know: dogs, bourbon, dirty blues. I even played her some of my Little Junior Parker and His Blue Flames records, 'Mystery Train' and 'Love My Baby.' The woman was unmoved."

"Queenie and I went to Hot Springs," Archie said. "On our honeymoon, you know. We stayed in the famous old hotel there, the Arlington, did all the famous old things. Bathhouse Row and played the ponies at Oaklawn."

There didn't seem to be anything to say to that. He seemed to be very far away from us. He seemed to be back there, young and in love with Queenie, and her with him.

So Donnie said to me, "You broke it off, then."

"We decided, let's say, on separate honeymoons. I really did go to Dublin, the pub tour. McDaids and Neary's, Mulligan's and Doyle's, the Gravediggers, the Confession Box. O'Neill's on Suffolk and O'Neills on Pearse. On it went. There a week. I'm told it rained every day."

"She go on her cruise?"

"Guess so, don't know. But we did have a proper parting first. Amicable, as it happened. We'd found the one thing we agreed on—the two of us, no business getting married."

"Even so, to come that close. Do you ever think of her, Charley?"

"I do, sometimes. Good woman, as women go. Lovely voice."

"Like song, you said."

"Well, almost."

And then on we drank, and in the absence of song, we sang. We sang blues laments that were sad and country weepers that were sadder still. We did not, even as drunk as we were, attempt a soul strut. Instead, the old man, Archie the barkeep, crooned just a little, and Donnie Ferriday, the jukebox repairman, made like an old out-of-tune horn. Your man was on harmony vocals and foot stomps. Somewhere in the crevices of the old joint, a cricket may well have joined in.

## MORNING BRINGS HEALING ON HEELS OF HANGOVER

Donnie slept in a back booth of the bar. He woke up the next morning with a hangover of mythic scale. But hell, it was nothing a cup of Archie's coffee could not remedy. He poured a stout cup and added a packet of Goody's, like you would powdered creamer.

And so, inside of an hour, Donnie was crouched again before the old machine, the sleeves of his sweater, an old green cardigan from the Goodwill store where he scoured for records, pushed up just shy of the elbows. He did not seem to feel the drafty cold of the old joint or hear the noisy silence of it. He had an assortment of new tubes and wires, screws, switches, and black tape, all arranged on a bar rag he'd gotten from Archie. He said maybe he'd have to replace everything but that ancient grease, that gunk.

He took one breath and exhaled two. He reached inside the jukebox with his left hand and put his fingers to a clump of wires, as if checking its pulse, and with his right hand began loosening one of those old tubes; a single ghost stirred, just slightly.

The healing had begun.

WORLD-RECORD ATTEMPT FAILS; BAD, BAD WHISKEY TO BLAME

I didn't hear from Donnie for two weeks after, during which I wrote, or tried to, the start of his story. There was much crumpled paper and some of the old "head, meet wall" routine, and once, as a diversion, I tried to sail a 78 rpm record of "Bad, Bad Whiskey" by Amos Milburn and his Aladdin Chickenshackers from the front porch, through the front door, on through the living room and kitchen, out the window over the kitchen sink, and then outside, into the backyard and onto the spindle of my old portable record player, which rested on a card table. It would require a master's touch, God's timing, some dark magic, and so very much bourbon, to pull off such a feat. The record player was plugged in, with an extension cord running across the yard into the kitchen, as if I somehow expected success. Or anyway, was bracing for it. A show of hubris? Or maybe it was just the old Boy Scout in me, being prepared.

I positioned myself down the sidewalk, so as to raise the degree of difficulty to an Olympian level. I went into a sort of ready position, a semi-crouch that must have made the neighbors, if they were looking on, think I'd finally gone full-on batty.

I counted down. I let loose. My form was good—it felt so. I had force and follow-through. And the record sailed. It sailed yea wide of the front door, hitting a window and breaking same. There was a mad crash, sounded like a great splintering of the world. There was broken glass and shellac all about.

I blamed God, and Amos Milburn.


DREAMING HEADLINE DREAMS

I went back to writing, back to banging my head against the wall. I dreamed headline dreams. I drank some more bad, bad whiskey. Days passed and I hadn't written a usable word, but at least I had a title.

I went to see Donnie Ferriday. I walked there. He'd moved out of his place and taken a room in a big, two-story house on East Booker, over near Crump Stadium. He was already looking to get the hell out of there. The owner was a Midtown eccentric and fancied the house as some sort of artists' salon, where writers and painters, sculptors and even free-jazz drummers could repair, finding refuge, the spark of inspiration, and the makings of a hot meal. The Midtown eccentric traveled widely and was seldom at home, and from every trip returned home hoping to find the place bursting with color and song and all other manner of art, or at least not burned to the foundation. There was one artist there the day I visited—a cellist, down from Minnesota, who said he was writing an operetta. He said he was traveling the country, seeking out the sites of terrific disasters and setting them to music. He had been to locations of mine cave-ins, train wrecks, plane crashes, bridge collapses, duels, spontaneous combustions, and assassinations. He had been to great metropolises and little burgs, from the great northeast to the golden west, the five boroughs of New York City to a town in California called Spit, or Spat, he could not remember which. But he said Memphis, Home of the Blues, was the best yet, so rich it was in calamity and sadness, and death, just generally. "And yet," he said, "and yet ..." It was for his cello to say the rest. He took up the thing and sawed a few lines of the operetta for us, there on the front porch of the big, old house, with a little boy from the neighborhood at the bottom of the stoop, all of us listening as he played.

What little I knew about operettas is that they were light pieces, sprightly in nature. He said his was about the Yellow Fever epidemic of 1878. But it was an operetta, sure enough. Notes danced and floated, none so much as touching the floor; a mosquito would have been dizzied by the sound. The little boy seemed to be trying to resist the urge to dance, off the stoop and onto the sidewalk and out into the Memphis morn.

Then he did dance, just a little. He seemed to forget, or not know, that the piece concerned a plague on Memphis, and that it killed some five thousand souls and very nearly took the city itself. Maybe he thought the Yellow Fever was just the name of some old dance craze and that he might, with his singular moves, bring it back. He rattled his young bones, he shook his proper little self. Eyes closed and smiling, he was off somewhere else now, moved, transported, delivered.

Maybe this was the point of it all, I thought. To take whatever escape is handy from the hard times, to lose yourself, go long, get lost. Dance the dance of death like it's The Monkey or The Dog. Or maybe the cellist from Minnesota was daft, or had a condition that affected his cognitive discernment of happy and sad; I wondered if such a condition, if such existed, would be a burden or relief? Could you catch it like the croup? Did they have pills for it? Gum or a patch?

I looked over at the cellist. He was crying as he sawed that happy tune of death and rot. When he stopped, I asked were they tears of joy. He looked at me and said, "No."

We left the cellist on the porch, crying onto his instrument. The little boy had joined a neighborhood game of Terrorize Some Old Person with Whatever's Handy; a little gang of them were waving twigs and branches at a woman carrying a bag of groceries down the sidewalk. So much for being transported by art, altered by it. Modern society has the attention span of—what was I saying?

The old woman reached in the bag and pulled out an orange and heaved it at the boys. It missed, badly, but they chased the thing down and started a new game with it. Terrorize Each Other with an Orange, I think it was called. The old woman shuffled up the sidewalk and disappeared inside some hovel. Smart lady.

Donnie and I walked over to a soul food place across from Crump Stadium. We ate catfish and greens—well, he had greens. I got fries as my side, as ever the healthy eater.

"So how the hell did you end up at that house?"

"The owner—I'd fixed some of his jukeboxes. He has a collection of them, in a building he rents on Union. It was never anything complicated. They're not real complicated machines, you know, the old ones. You've seen them. Hell, you could fix them. It's mostly tubes and grease, and wires, of course—making sure the right ones touch and the wrong ones don't. Swap out a switch, like that. But hell, this guy. He said I was a true artist. A healer. I'd fix a jukebox and he'd play a song, and you'd think it was me singing it. He was—"

"A sweet guy."

"Delusional."

"I don't think you can be sweet without being delusional, at least a little."

"Anyway, he said to come stay at his house if I ever needed a place." Donnie shrugged and ate some greens. It was like he was taking a bite of swamp. He smiled. "I needed a place. But Jesus, you can't get a second's rest. Last week there was a brass band. But they didn't raise near the ruckus the poet did."

"You've got to watch those poets. I've always said that. So what happened with your place? Business gotten that bad?"

"Christ, Charley. Business was bad when it was good. Lately it's all but gone away. I'm getting out—not that anybody'll notice."

"I'd like to buy your business, Donnie."

"There's nothing to buy and you're nearly broke, yourself."

"Not a lot of haggling, then, huh?"

"Business is not for sale, Charley. It dies with me. Sorry."

"Well, no bother. The stagecoach has been calling. Seasonal hiring only, but it's something."

"You're a writer, Charley."

"So?"

"So write."

"I'll write your story, Donnie. I've already started, in fact."

"Why the hell would you do that?"

"I've got a title."

"Do you, now?"

"*Tales of Ancient Grease.*"

He smiled. "That's a good title, Charley. I like it. But I wouldn't want to read it, having lived it. I don't know why the hell anybody else would, either. No offense."

"It's about all the big, old, enduring themes, Donnie—work, family, identity, the heart in conflict with itself, soul songs about the dark end of the street. Well, it will be once I've written it."

He rolled his eyes.

"Ah, you know what they say," I said. "Writing's ninety percent title and ten percent bourbon." I said it like I believed it.

We finished lunch. The poor bastard without a job paid and the poor bastard whose business was losing money every day it stayed open let me do it.

"You can crash at my place, Donnie."

"I'm leaving, Charley."

"Where to?"

"Missouri. Up where my wife and her new husband live, with my son."

"You going to try to win her back, your wife?"

"No, not that, Charley. She's happy. He's a good man. They love each other. They match. But I figure I can be a good father to my boy, see him when I can—when I'm allowed. I want to be there. Be a decent father, and a good ex-husband. Hell of a thing to aspire to, huh?"

"Hell, Donnie, to aspire at all …"

"Yeah, small steps, you know."

"What'll you do for work? Open a jukebox repair shop in ol' Mizzou?"

"Christ, no. I'm going to get a regular job, doing regular things. Something with my hands."

I looked at my own. I took one and gave Donnie Ferriday a pat on the back. I said he was a good man and hoped to hell he could be that decent father, that good ex-husband. I said I'd miss the poor bastard.

"What about you, Charley. What's going to become of you?"

"I don't know. I had my mind set on writing your story."

"Hell, Charley."
"What?"
"Write your own."

# 5

# Death of a showboat

The big man waved as he walked the length of the barroom toward me. "Brother," he said. That boom of a voice, that paw of a hand. Ah, Winston. It had been too long. I was sitting at a small table in back, under a signed team picture of the old Memphis Showboats football team. I knew he would appreciate the symbolism, without calling it that, and not make too much of the fact that the picture had long faded, and most of the signatures, too. I took a drink of beer and raised the bottle in greeting. Hell fella and all. I wondered how we'd look to each other. Faded, at best, I guessed.

I'd had an uneventful few weeks. I'd achieved a sort of stasis, which is to say I'd been an utter load. Then my old high school friend called. I hadn't seen him in a few years. He said he needed to talk to me. We agreed to meet at an old haunt called the Old Haunt. Well, we used to call it that. It was a dive bar over off Cleveland, down an alley and up a dead-end street. I'd tell you where, exactly, but then I'd have to buy you a drink.

We played football together at White Station. That is, Winston played football and I stood on the sidelines and wondered when the game would finally end so we could go and drink some beers, Winston and I, and usually Doral, his little brother, and talk about talking to some girls while the stars of the team, the quarterback and wide receivers and running backs—the "skill-position players," they were called; Christ, like all the rest of us were cavemen or something, evolved just enough to learn a three-point stance—were off doing things with girls other than talking. I had only a vague idea what those things might be.

We were linemen together. That's how we got to be friends, unlikely as it was. I didn't even like football, failed to see the point of it entirely, except as a sort of rude theater of life in which some boys and men were cast as gods and others as mules. (And girls and women as things, scenery, goddesses for the gods.) I secretly wanted the linemen to rise up one day at practice and overthrow the skill-position players and the coaches, lash them all to the goalposts and then, I don't know, just go off and hit the buffet at Golden India. Fucking football. If somebody asked me why I played, I'd have told them I liked the idea of disappearing into a uniform and sticking a helmet on my head, so I looked pretty much like the fellow next to me and the one next to him. Or maybe, somewhere deep in my subconscious, down in the cellar of the thing, I was seeking the approval of my father, who loved football almost as much as he loved his damn war movies. But nobody ever asked. I'm not sure anybody even noticed I was on the team. That was fine, too.

Winston was good. He played offense and defense, both. He was all-metro, and then second-team all-conference at Mississippi State, and then he played a few years in the NFL before his fourth or fifth or twenty-eighth concussion, and then even the team said he couldn't play anymore. Your head about had to fall off your shoulders before the team wouldn't send you back out there. But that's not what all this was about. This was about Winston and that old boy.

That's what Winston always called him. I'd about forgotten he had a proper name, until I saw it in the newspaper, a week before Winston called, under the headline about a body dragged up out of Moon Lake, an hour south of Memphis, in Coahoma County, Mississippi.

I smiled at my old friend. I stood up and we bear-hugged. I disappeared into him. He looked about like the old Winston, more or less. No, more *and* less: walked with a bit of a limp, stood with a slight stoop, but still in good shape, and somehow handsome where he hadn't been before. He'd grown comfortable with that big body of his, I guess. I didn't know if he was of sound mind, after all those concussions, but the lights all seemed to be on. There were maybe two or three that flickered. But hell, that's all of us.

"It's damn good to see you, Winston."

"You, too, brother."

He never called me by my name, just brother. Winston called everybody he liked his brother, except his own. They were more than that to each other. He was Doral's idol and protector and more a father to him than their actual one. Hell, he was father and mother, both, and a damned sight better at it than the pair who, yes really, named their boys after brands of cigarettes.

Doral was slight and a bit slow but good fun, a real joker. I was surprised he wasn't here with Winston. They were always together. It had been a few years since I'd seen them, but I couldn't imagine anything had changed. It was like there was just one shadow between them—Winston's; Doral wouldn't have wanted to be anywhere else.

"How's he doing? He still working for the county?"

"Yeah. He's good. He'll be here later. I had him drop me off and then sent him on some errands. He knows all I'm going to tell you—he's the only one who does. I figured it'd be easier to tell it all, without him interrupting, you know."

"He's a good guy."

Winston smiled. "Hell, he's got a girlfriend—and a black eye. She's a rough thing, a boxer. She's been on a couple undercards down at the casinos. Well, she popped him one. They were out drinking, over to Murphy's, I think, and Doral told her she was heaven sent. But you know how you can't hardly understand him sober when he gets to going, and he wasn't sober, and his girl, she thought he called her heavy set. Well, that's when she popped him."

He was still laughing about Doral and Doral's girl, as he sat down opposite me. "Angel's her name," he said. "Stout gal, hair trigger of a temper. She popped him in the eye and he fell to a knee. So Doral, never the quickest thinker, you know, fooled us all this time. While he was down there, he thought, hell, I'm down on one knee already, I'll propose to her. He figured that'd be the one way he could get back up without getting popped again. Leave it to Doral—finally does some quick thinking, and

138

damned if it ain't by proposing to a girl he's only dated for a month, who can flat stomp his ass. But you know Doral. And he is sweet on the girl. So there you go."

"What'd his girl say? She say yes?"

"Said she'd have to think on it. But they're still going out, and Doral's working on his—what you call it?"

"Enunciation? Rope-a-dope?"

Winston shrugged and smiled. "The both of them, I guess, brother."

We laughed. We sat and drank our beers and talked some more small talk. The jukebox played a song off an old Alex Chilton album from the Eighties, the one where it sounds like he's fronting the house band at a strip club. "Take It Off," the name of the song. It's a little number about free will and false eye lashes.

Listening to Winston talk, I remembered those football Friday nights. I was his backup and almost never had to play. I was tall but skinny, not built for the trenches. I guess they figured I'd be safe as a backup to Winston, who hardly needed one. I spent every minute staring off in one direction or another, anything to avoid watching the game itself. I kept my helmet on, always. It was easier to ignore the action that way, and not risk getting yelled at by one of the coaches. A little eye contact was all they needed. That would call to mind what a fucking, little shit-ass you were to them. The coaches all yelled. They'd yell at tackling dummies and water coolers, when there was no player handy. They'd yell at the ghosts of former players. If they were yelling at me, they'd have realized I was on the team, and I didn't see any good coming of that.

I stared across the field at the other team's fans, watching them sit as quiet as could be for the longest stretches, and then, all of the sudden, they'd be jolted to life. It was like fireworks at a funeral. What a strange fucking game, football. I think it explains America; if somebody hasn't said that already, put me down for it.

And I stared at the cheerleaders of both teams, looking for one I might have the nerve or desire to talk to. But I never found one. They all seemed like some strange other life form to me, like one of us had landed on the wrong planet. I figured it had to be them; how could somebody be so happy all the time? They were smiling and kicking up their long legs and shouting the sporting version of hallelujah. Addendum: Football can't fully explain America without long-legged cheerleaders.

I'd stare at the band, too, all in their dapper uniforms with their plumes and their horns and their grave faces like it really was a funeral out there, and they were to try, somehow, to uplift the grieving masses with their brassy songs and precise footwork.

Four seasons on the team and I don't think I ever saw an entire play. I think I even missed the rare ones I was part of. It all seemed like madness to me, out there on the field, once the ball was snapped. I figured it must have been like war, only without the killing or protests for it to stop. There were protests over football, of course, but much later, and only briefly. A year or two after I met with Winston, everybody, even the president, was suddenly talking about how dangerous football was to the human head. There was a national debate about the safety of the game, whether we ought to let kids play it, whether it might someday be banned. Looking back, the backlash against football had serious momentum—for a couple of days. People loved the game too much to really change it. They loved everything about it, truth be told: the savagery and pageantry, the butting heads and the long legs, the way it really did, even more than war, explain America. Hell, it *was* war, with beer commercials. Somebody surely has said that before.

But mostly I hated the game because of how it put some players on pedestals, to preen, and others in cages, to work themselves into violent frenzies and then be let out on Friday night or Saturday afternoon or all day on Sunday. Fucking football.

I did write up stories for the school paper, though. My calling, of course. Budding reporter and all. I took the boxscores and imagined the rest. I'd usually include some reference to Winston, as if a lineman, of all things, had been crucial to the outcome, the star of the game. One time he really was, and that's what this was all about, sort of.

*

"They pulled that old boy from Moon Lake," Winston said. "I guess you know that part already."

"I read about it, yeah."

"Hell, I thought you probably wrote it, brother."

"You don't know, do you? They let me go, Winston. It was months ago."

"The hell they do that for? You were good."

I guess he took it on faith I was a good reporter, just because I was his friend or because he figured I had to be good at something; he knew I wasn't but a fucking, little shit-ass at football.

"It's that whole newspapers-are-dying thing, Winston. They've been letting us go, waves at a time, for a few years now. It's how they try to save themselves. It's all they know to do. They give us a check, and the boot. I lasted longer than some. I like to think it's because I was pretty good. But near as I could tell it didn't matter whether you were good or only so-so or outright not worth a damn. They quit making the distinction some time back. But, hell, the not-worth-a-damn, they're running the place. Maybe they always were." I shrugged and took a drink of beer. "You don't want to hear all this."

He just said, "Well, shit. So much for that plan."

"What do you mean?"

"I was going to confess to you."

"I was a reporter, Winston, not a priest. They're kind of opposite things altogether."

"Well, I don't know any priests, brother. I know you."

"You wanted to confess—what?—murder to me?"

"That was the plan, brother."

He didn't even need to drop his voice to say all this. It was just the two of us, at that back table, under that faded picture of the old Memphis Showboats, and Alex Chilton on the jukebox telling his lady friend to take off her wig.

"Confess? And knowing I'd have to do something about it—write a story, talk to the cops, all that."

"You'd get a big, what they call it? Scoop. Hell, yeah. You'd get a big one of those."

"Goddamn, Winston. Did you really kill that old boy?"

∗

He finished his beer and raised his hand for another. The jukebox played a Replacements song, one they recorded a mile or two away, at Ardent Studios, over on Madison. The song was called "Alex Chilton." It was a love song to the band's musical hero, the best song on my favorite album of theirs, but now it just reminded me that Alex was dead now. I didn't know him, just saw him play a couple of times, long after his days in that great band Big Star. I liked that he didn't care to be what people wanted him to be. He sang what he wanted, and fuck-all what his fans or the radio or the record companies wanted. What some people saw as an almost cunning knack for sabotaging his career, I recognized as that particularly ornery strain of Memphis-style artistic integrity. It's some potent shit; I sometimes wonder what would have happened if Jerry Lee Lewis had had a little less of it, and Elvis a little more. I think Alex had just the right amount, somehow. Now he was dead and gone, and fronting strip-club house bands in heaven. Not even God could tell Alex Chilton what to sing.

I smiled at the thought. I said for the bartender to make it two. Then I asked Winston again if he'd killed that old boy.

"There's a whole long story," he said. "I need to tell it all, if you ain't got nowhere to be."

I looked at him and smiled—*ain't got nowhere to be.* It was like a koan or something. Or the story of my life after the newspaper sacked me.

"I could find you another reporter to tell it to, if you want to get your ass arrested," I said. "I could make a call."

"Nah, brother. I wanted to tell somebody I knew. Somebody I trusted. I wanted to tell somebody who was there when it all began, that night with me and that old boy. You remember the play, right?"

It was out on what they call the flat, on our side of the field, not five yards from where I stood on the sideline. The flat—people who love football talk about the parts of the field as if they were sacred patches of old battlefields, like the flat or the trenches at Fairgrounds stadium, where we played our home games because White Station didn't have its own field, were like the Hornet's Nest or the Bloody Pond of Shiloh. So, the flat, on the home side of the field. Pretty much right in front of me, impossible to miss, but I missed it, like I missed every other play. I just heard it—Christ, the sound it made. I can hear it, still, like an electric splat or something. It's all anybody talked about in school the next week.

It was senior year. We were playing Ridgeway, our rival. That old boy was their star quarterback, already committed to play at Alabama. It was a trick play, a fake end-around. That detail seems to matter to some people, so I relate it here. It was late in the game. I remember that—I'd stare at the scoreboard, too, but not to look at the score. I watched the clock, to see if it was time to go and drink beer and be ignored by girls.

So the end came around and the old boy faked a handoff and he rolled left himself and turned the corner to go downfield. The play must have fooled everybody on our team but Winston, because it was just the two of them out there alone on that patch of field they call the flat. That wasn't even where Winston, a lineman, was supposed to be. But he knew to be there, somehow.

People said everything stopped for half a second. That old boy froze—not because he was scared of Winston. He was fucking with him, for the usual reason people who are fancied stars fuck with people who aren't—because he could. And another reason, too: because Winston was big enough to crush that old boy, but not fast enough to catch him. They both knew it, too. Winston told me later that old boy looked almost glad to see him, just for somebody good and big to fuck with. He said that old boy stopped that half a second to give Winston a chance at guessing, because guessing was the one chance Winston had: Would he juke and go right or bob and go left? Winston swears that old boy smiled, even—he did, too, in the school-newspaper version I wrote up later.

But Winston didn't guess right or guess left. He didn't guess at all. He went straight at that old boy before the old boy could decide himself. It wasn't like time started up again. It was more like Winston punched the face of a great clock with his fist, and created some new reality entirely, the Time of the Linemen. He hit that old boy head-on. He hit him so hard that old boy spun half around and started running the wrong way. Even I was watching it by now. That old boy got ten yards toward his own goal line before one of his teammates caught him and tried turning him around. They got all tangled up, those two. By then, that old boy couldn't run a step. He just sort of crumpled in a bone pile on the field, with the teammate standing over him, nudging him with the toe of his cleat to see if he was still alive. He was, but he had no wits about him, and he'd pissed himself, they said. He was hauled off the field on a stretcher. It was all on the TV Action News that night and in the newspaper the next morning.

The old boy got his wits back, most of them, after a few days. But he was never the same player again. Winston knocked the hot-shit out of him. By the end of the season, he was sitting on the bench with some injury everybody said was fake.

*

We made it to the state semifinals. Winston took a blonde cheerleader to a big school dance. They walked in with her on his shoulders, White Station legend has it. It really was the Time of the Linemen, there for a few crazy weeks.

He smiled, remembering all this. He said, "Best days of my life, you know? I know that's some sad shit to even think about, I do. But hell, brother, your best days got to come sometime, don't they, lest they don't come at all."

"Did you just use the word *lest*, Winston?"

"I did it for you, my brother. You seem kind of low."

"Well, however you say it, that's some true wisdom there, Winston, my man."

"People always think you're dumb if you're big, you know."

"I never did."

"They think big's all the hell you are. You can be tall and smart but not *big* and smart. You can be big and funny. That's OK. They'll laugh at anything you say—like a cow telling a joke."

"You've thought about all this."

"You ever see a big ol' cow in the field didn't look like he had something deep on his mind, only you don't know what?"

"I guess."

"Well then."

He raised his bottle and then put it back down without taking a drink.

"Now you look a little down," I said.

"Nah, brother. Just talking, saying shit. Anyway, you play a little football, people look at you a little different, even if you were just a big, dumb lineman that never touched the damn ball once. I had that, at least. I sure as hell played."

I shrugged and smiled at the big lug. "So what was on your mind, those days?"

"Girls, brother—like you and everybody else but the ones that didn't have to wonder."

"You've become a wise soul, Winston, I swear." I wondered if all those concussions had knocked some wires and tubes loose in a good way. "You're damned near a philosopher, these days."

"Hell, people only want to ask me about playing in the NFL. They want to see the ring I got when the team won the Super Bowl, even though I couldn't play—had a concussion so bad I thought two and two was cream gravy. And they want to ask about that time with me and All-Pro Jones, that day in Kansas City. They want to know did I really hit him so hard he spoke French like a French girl. Shit, brother, I want to tell them about that school dance, me and that blonde cheerleader. You remember her?"

"They all looked alike to me."

"I think that was the point. Or hell, the rule. And they only had, like, three names between them. There were a couple, three Michelles and a few of Jessicas. Mine was a Cindy."

"What the hell did you two even talk about, Winston? I mean, when she came down from your shoulders and the cheering stopped and it was just you two?" I wanted to say, "What do a caveman boy and an alien girl even say, without a common language between them?"

But he wasn't listening. He was staring at the wall, at that team picture of the old Showboats, the faded faces, the faded names. He was smiling.

✳

More beers. More Memphis songs on the jukebox. Songs about smoke and goodbyes, girls and devils. The jukebox was on a Lucero jag now. Love that band. I figured we'd get to Winston killing that old boy when we got to it.

"You remember that night, brother?" he finally said.

"The game? Listen, I've got to tell you, Winston. I never saw the games. I never looked. I hate football. I always did."

"Shit, not football, brother. Hell, I never watched a game I didn't play in. I mean the night of the dance."

"I didn't go, remember?"

"Shit, that's right. You had that condition, what was it?"

I laughed. I'd forgotten. "I said I was having an existential crisis. It's not really a condition."

"It sort of is."

"I guess so, yeah."

"I offered to set you up with my little sister, Cammie. Sweet girl. She liked you. Thought you were hung like the moon—ha!"

"She was in, like, sixth grade."

Winston hooted. I smiled.

(Yes, it's true, even parents as lousy as Winston and Doral's couldn't bring themselves to name a girl baby after a brand of cigarettes. But then, Cammie may well have been short for camouflage.)

He said, "Hell, why didn't you just ask that girl you were always going on about it. The hell was her name? Started with an F."

"Emily?"

"That's it."

"She was my cousin, Winston."

"Well, shit, brother, Cammie was my little sister."

✳

Ah, my existential crisis.

I didn't mention it to my parents. My father wouldn't have known what the hell existential even meant, but if there wasn't gushing blood or exposed bones he wouldn't have thought it a crisis. I didn't tell my mother because she'd have believed me.

✳

Another couple of beers, another couple of Lucero songs on the jukebox. Songs about whiskey and tattoos and little silver hearts. Songs about waking up on the floor—but hell, to wake up at all, right?

Winston was rambling, but I wasn't going anywhere. If I'd still been a reporter, I'd have been pushing him to get to the part where he murdered that old boy—worried he'd lose his nerve before he got there. But I was just a poor bastard without prospects, drinking off my severance in a dive bar on a Thursday afternoon at the tired end of a Memphis winter. I didn't have nowhere to be, like the man said. I went for another round.

I figured if I was drunk enough, and the music was sad and loud enough, I wouldn't dwell on what seemed to be staring me down, just now: that my old football days were a metaphor for my life, that I'd spent it standing on the sidelines of the thing, watching others have their best days and worst days and all those others in between. There was Winston—he'd done things, he'd lived. He'd played in the NFL and had concussions and worn a blonde cheerleader on his shoulder. He'd been a father to his little brother. He'd killed a man and come to confess. The hell had I done? Written a bunch of stories about shit other people had done. Now I didn't even do that. I didn't do anything.

Then I did begin to dwell on all that, but Winston saved me. He told me the rest of the story. I remembered parts of it. I remembered how that old boy—Bobby Lee DeMent was his name—stole Winston's cheerleader girlfriend, and how Winston shrugged it off because he knew it never would have lasted, anyway. And I remembered how that old boy then stole Winston's car and parked it in the big yard out front of East High School on Poplar, with a sledgehammer and a sign that said three whacks for a dollar. Now, this bothered Winston a little, for he loved the old junker, knew and understood it like he never could that cheerleader. But still, he figured that old boy, who would never play college football or become the king of Tuscaloosa, Alabama, had a right to revenge and he must be close to getting it.

Then nothing happened for a few years. This was the pattern—nothing happened and then something did. That old boy must have had to ruminate on what revenge he'd concoct next, if indeed old boys ruminate and concoct and put that level of actual thought and reflection into what they do.

So we all graduated and went our separate ways, mostly. I went to college to learn to be a newspaperman, which seemed, even at the time, like going to church to learn bartending, but there you go. I went to Arkansas on a little bit of an academic scholarship. Winston went to Mississippi State on a football ride. He met a girl there. She wasn't a cheerleader. She wasn't even in college. She was the daughter of a maintenance man at the football stadium. She waited tables at a restaurant where Winston and the other linemen ate. They got on. They stayed together through the good and bad, the NFL and the concussions and Super Bowl Sunday and more concussions. Winston said at the worst of them, those concussions, she'd coo in his ear. He said it didn't do much, strictly speaking, for the concussion, but it took his mind off it—took his mind off his mind, I think he was saying.

"So … your wife."

"Bess—an old country name, you know. I called her Bessie. No cheerleader ever was called Bessie, I don't think." He lifted his bottle and smiled, fairly beamed at it. "She was real. She was country, even living in the city. Well, Starkville. She was, what you call, earthy. You know what I mean, brother?"

"I do."

"I wonder sometimes if that's why I married her."

"Why's that, Winston?"

"Because she was an earthy, l'il country girl named Bessie, daughter of a stadium maintenance man."

I puzzled it out. Those old reporter synapses still had a little blind-squirrel acorn juice left yet. "You mean to say you married a girl you thought that old boy wouldn't steal?"

We both stared at our bottles. I could not have told you what the jukebox was playing. It might have been hymns or grand opera, for all I knew in that small moment.

"I think that sometimes, yeah."

I thought a little more. "So the last thing you wanted was to lose her," I said. "Well, shit, Winston. That's some true love there."

"Kind of a fucked-up way to go about it, brother."

"Well."

"But anyway, he stole her. My wife. Bess. Bessie."

*

It was probably more happenstance than wild-hair notion this time. They all ended up working at FedEx, like every third person in Memphis.

"He stole her—wooed her and stole her, sure did. They worked together in the main hub. I was over at Hacks Cross, the offices there. Seems they thought I had some kind of junior management potential. I think they just liked my football stories. The big man sure as hell did. I met him once. He like to never let me go and get back to work."

"So crime of opportunity, pretty much, on that old boy's part."

"Crime, hmm. You think about it, brother. It's the one thing a man can steal from another, free and clear, and can't a thing be done. A man can't go to the cops and report his wife stolen. A wife ain't a boat."

I said I guessed not. I'd had neither wife nor boat and couldn't speak to the legal similarities thereof or herein.

I thought to move the story along. I said, "So then you killed him, that old boy."

"Nah, hell. That was a couple of years ago."

"You didn't kill him for stealing your wife?"

"Seemed a screwy kind of thing to do after all those years, to kill him just when he'd gotten even."

"But not even. Not yet."

"That's right, brother. You know it. He still had one more thing to do."

So Winston told the rest of it. He told about how she left him for that old boy, and how, after that old boy cast her aside, Winston and Bess couldn't quite bring themselves to get back together. "I would, but not her," Winston said. "She thought she'd shamed herself, shamed us. I said there were worse things to live with than shame and she said like what and I said I don't know, lots of things, and she said name two." He sighed. "If I hadn't had forty-two concussions or whatever, maybe I could have thought of an answer before she walked away." And he told how he quit FedEx and took what was left of his football money and pretty much disappeared, or the nearest thing to it: opened a bait shop down south of Memphis, almost to the state line. He thought that might as well have been East Pluto or Stuporville, Oklahoma, for steering clear of that old boy—because one more time and Winston really would kill him.

And so it happened, that one more time. Whether it was happenstance or wild-hair notion this time, Winston couldn't say, but that old boy came to know Winston had opened a bait shop, and it became the latest thing he had to take from him. It was, whether that old boy Bobby Lee DeMent intended it or not, the last thing.

✻

"It was in the back room, what I used to call my office," Winston said. "Back room of the bait shop he swindled me out of. Damn. I was some all-league dumbass, day I let that happen."

I didn't push for details. Hell, I wasn't a reporter anymore. I didn't need to know about how much of a dumbass you have to be to get swindled out of a bait shop. Let a man have a little dignity when he's down—it's kind of like my Golden Rule.

But then Winston told it, anyway. He said, "That old boy had this friend pose as some kind of agent, representing these developers. Said they had big plans for that strip of nothing out there, almost to the state line. Said it was valuable because it was as close to the Mississippi casinos as you could get and still be in Tennessee. Said I could buy in cheap on the new thing they were planning, which they couldn't talk about just yet, all hush-hush, you know, zoning approvals, non-disclosure bullshit, blah-blah. Sounded kind of screwy, selling out and then buying in, but hell

... I don't know. Doral, he thought maybe they were going to build a football stadium down there and snatch the fucking Titans away from Nashville. Well, that was ridiculous. But I think it was Doral's way of saying he wished his big brother, his hero and all, was doing something more than selling worms and bootlegging a little beer. I told the man yes.

"So now the bait shop belonged to that old boy. My nemesis, you know. I think he bought it figuring he'd shut it down right quick, just to piss me off even more. But then I think he realized it wasn't bad, having a bait shop. It's about the nearest thing to not working, brother.

"So he kept it open. He showed up every day and opened the place. I watched him do it—watched for the longest time. I never walked in until this one day, along about evening." He stopped and sighed and then started up again. "It was getting to be closing time. He was in the back room. He didn't hear me come in, had the radio on. They were giving the weather. Radio said rain. I remember that. I walked in that back room. I had this stone in my hand and he had his back to me. But I didn't just conk him one. Stone about yea big, and him over there puttering. Radio played a song now. Modern Country bullshit. That old boy had no better taste in music than that stone in my hand.

"Then I dropped it. I didn't need it to kill that old boy. Had my hands for that. I dropped that stone to get his attention. *Thud.* He turned. We looked at each other a full minute, seemed like. It was like that night all over again, that night in high school, at Fairgrounds stadium, only without a crowd and lights and the band and cheerleaders, and you, brother, there on the sidelines, in case I needed backup."

He reached over and gave me a pat with his paw. I tried to give him a smile but couldn't, quite. Then I said something I'd never said as a newspaperman.

"You sure you want to tell me this?"

"Does seem kind of a waste, you not being a reporter anymore. But yeah. I do."

"All right, then."

He took a drink of beer and then looked away without really looking at anything at all. Then he smiled a smile of something like wonderment.

"It was the damnedest thing," he said, finally. "I was staring at the high school version of that old boy, and I reckon he was staring back at the high school version of me. Hot-shit quarterback, Alabama-bound, and big ol' me."

"Fucking with you, all over again."

"He was, like you say, fucking with me all over again. He was, brother. So I came at him, all of a sudden, like I did that night. Only I'd lost a step. Or maybe he took me for one of those ponies with just the one trick, because he moved, just in time. He knew to expect it."

"So then what happened?"

"I went crashing through all manner of shit, cut myself up, my leg got bent a funny way." He smiled. "May have gotten myself another one of those fucking concussions, only in the knee this time."

I laughed and then I didn't.

"I guess by the time you had your wits about you, that old boy had himself a gun," I said.

I just knew it, having heard, in my newspaper days, a million stories and their million variations about the sort of altercations that rise to the level of newspaper-worthy. There's nearly always a gun handy. That's as American as football and cheerleaders.

"It's like you were there, brother."

"I hate to have missed it, Winston, being as I was your backup."

"I might could've used you, but I don't know for what. Two against one still ain't good numbers when the one has a gun." Then he smiled again. "But I realized, it wasn't just any gun. It was mine—the one I'd had in the drawer of that table I called a desk, in that back room I called an office. I forgot it, left it there, and he found it. So nah, brother, I didn't need backup. Because I knew."

"The gun wasn't loaded?"

"Oh, hell, gun was loaded. Gun was always fucking loaded." He grinned. "It just didn't always shoot. It'd jam a lot of the time."

"But not *every* time."

"Well, no, but life's odds, brother."

"So then what happened?" I sounded like a broken record on a busted jukebox, but it was the best time I'd had in ages. I was beginning to think: I could write the hell out of this story.

"Everything slowed down, like that night on the football field. He was in control, again—thought he was. And I liked letting him think it. Because I was just some big dumb animal to him. So we stood there and stared. Radio played on. More of that Modern Country bullshit. Singer singing about cold friends and old beer. I remember thinking, OK, well that's kind of funny. But it'd been better if it was David Allan Coe singing it. Or maybe Merle. Johnny Paycheck. I told the old boy that. He said to shut it. So I did, just to keep him thinking he was in control. Then the song ended and it was traffic and weather on the fives, or whatever it is they say in radio land. Then it was time."

✳

Winston had stopped talking. He was staring at that faded team picture of the old Memphis Showboats.

"My daddy, he'd take me and Doral to the Liberty Bowl, see them play," he said. "He wasn't much of a daddy but he did that much. He wanted me to go out for football, said I was big for a reason. We'd sit up high in the bleachers and he'd point down at the field, spilling half his beer on Doral, saying, 'Look a there, Winston. That's Reggie fucking White down there.'"

Winston laughed real big. He said, "Hell, brother, I wanted to be a pro rassler. Seemed like more fun to me."

"They had one of them on the team, too," I said. "Rassler." It felt good, just saying the word.

"Jerry Lawler?"

154

"Nah, not The King. That other one. Hell, I can't remember."

I knew it was Lex Luger, though he was just Larry something then. I just wanted to hear Winston run through a bunch of guesses. I wanted to hear those old names—Jimmy Hart the Mouth of the South and King Kong Bundy and the Moondogs. He ran through all those and some others, Dutch Mantel and the Fabulous Ones and Handsome Jimmy Valiant. I just wanted to hear the names and be a little kid again, for a few minutes. I wanted to revel in the age of elbow drops and piledrivers. A whole generation of Memphis snot-noses was raised on rasslin'— it taught us how to spell wrong and gave us a sense of metal-chair justice. Even bookish boys liked rasslin'.

"Lex Luger," I finally said. "I remembered."

"Lex Luger was a Showboat?"

"Hell, a lineman," I said. "Just like us."

"Shit, brother, you know every damn thing."

I didn't think knowing that Lex Luger played pro football in Memphis for a defunct team in a defunct league qualified as every damn thing. I didn't know a lick of calculus, or one tree from another. I didn't know women, or French, or what I was going to do next with my life. But what the hell?

"I read it in the newspaper," I said.

✳

Then Doral came through the door. I smiled and gave him a wave. "Hey, Charley man." "Hey, Doral." We bear-hugged. He gave Winston a back slap.

"Has you come to the good part, Winston?"

"Just about there, Doral."

Winston gave him a couple of bills for the jukebox. He played pretty much every Lucero song we'd heard already, every song about tattoos and whiskey, which is pretty much every Lucero song, subject-wise, but he also played one we hadn't heard yet, that one where Ben, the singer, sings about his little brother raising hell. I bet that was Doral's favorite song of all.

Then we listened as Winston told how, finally, he killed that old boy.

"I came at him, like before. The gun was no matter. He just assumed it would shoot and I knew it wouldn't, like as not. He didn't bother to jump aside because he knew what he knew—thought he did. I hit him hard and drove him against the concrete wall. I hit him hard as I hit All-Pro Jones, that day in Kansas City. It was like we hit that wall together and kept going. I believe the wall got the worst of it. Then I stopped. He slumped and I dropped him."

"Dead?"

"Sure as shit seemed it."

"Had he pulled the trigger?"

"He had. I looked."

"So it wasn't murder, Winston."

"I knew the gun wouldn't fire. Or pretty well knew."

"But still—" I didn't know what else to say. Yes, I did: "OK, so then what?"

✳

Winston told the rest. How he stood there for a couple of minutes and then remembered he had a joint in his shirt pocket. He said dope helped with the pain from all his old football injuries. He fired up that joint and smoked it, he said, but not for the pain. That would be later. For now, he needed to calm down. His mind was racing, he couldn't focus. He didn't know how much time passed, said it may have been ten minutes or an hour. He did have wits enough about him to turn off the damn radio, good man. "Modern Country bullshit," he said. "The fuck."

Then he did what I guess anybody would do. He did what he'd seen people do on TV. He wrapped the body of that old boy in a tarp, and then slung it up into the bed of his pickup truck.

156

"I went looking for a lake to dump him in," he said. "I drove over to Hook Lake, but there were a couple of old boys parked there, sitting on the tailgate drinking beers after a day of fishing. They waved. Knew me. I used to sell them bait, you know. And bootleg beer. So I went down across the state line, on down past Tunica, all the way to Moon Lake. It was well on dark now, but the moon was fat. There was nobody around, the place deserted. It all happened real slow and real fast, all at the same time. It was like football, that way. My ears were ringing, too, just like they did during a big game."

"But wait. What about—"

"What about what, brother?"

"The gun."

"Oh, that. He still had it in his hand. That old boy always did keep a good grip on things. You remember that night at Fairgrounds stadium, the football game? Hard as I hit him, he kept a hold of the ball. Ran backward, pissed his pants, and damned near fell down dead, but did not fumble. That's more'n All-Pro Jones could say."

"But your prints would be on the gun, too. From before." I was already thinking how Winston might get out from under this, the mitigating of the circumstances and such.

"Nah, not my prints. I kept it wiped clean, on account of if it was ever stolen, or some old boy grabbed it and tried to use it against me, there'd only be one set of prints on it."

"How'd you know to do that?"

"You own a bait shop, brother, you watch *a lot* of TV. Saw it on some old show, I guess," he said, and then: "So I hauled that old boy's body out of the truck. He was heavy as hell."

"That whole dead-weight thing." I felt like I was trying to stall him now, slow down the telling once he'd finally gotten around to it. I don't know why I wanted it to last, but I did. It was like time was going backward now. If it went far enough in that direction, maybe I'd be a newspaperman again.

"What dead-weight thing, brother?"

"How a dead body is heavier than a live one—or feels like it, at least. It's a scientific thing."

It's all I knew to say. I'd never killed anybody and I took C's in science.

"I guess, brother." He shrugged.

There was an old johnboat at the lake, so Winston said he loaded up the body and pushed off from the dock. He rowed out to the middle of the lake, remembered he had another joint, and so he fired it up. This time it was just for pleasure, he said.

"Ah, Moon Lake," I said. "Lots of ghosts there, Winston."

"What do you mean, brother?"

"Hell, that used to be the place to go. There was a famous club there, the Moon Lake Club, I think. People used to go to eat Kansas City steaks and lobster flown in from Maine or wherever. They'd drink, and dance, I guess, to hot jazz bands. Gamble, even. They had a casino there. Tennessee Williams wrote about it in some of his plays. His characters used to go on about it."

Winston just shrugged. He said, "Well, I didn't run across any ghosts or characters that night. Place was dead as that old boy." He smiled. "It was peaceful, though, I got to say. Just me and my rival, and him not saying a word. And then—"

He took a drink, he sighed. He looked at his little brother. I'd about forgotten Doral was even there. I'd never seen him so quiet. But he was rapt, listening to his hero tell the tale. It must have been like having a John Wayne movie for a big brother.

"And then what?" Doral said, though he must have heard it a hundred times.

"Alex Chilton had a pretty good song by that name," I said.

"Who had what, brother?" Winston said.

I don't know why I was still trying to slow down the story, now that there was a dead body in a boat.

"Alex Chilton," I said. "The singer, you know. He had a song called 'My Rival.' It's kind of a funny song, but kind of dark, too. Alex's rival has muscles and blond hair and drives a Triumph sports car."

But I did know why. Because I really didn't want it to end. I wanted it to go on forever.

"Did Alex's rival steal his girl?"

"He did, about a year before, the song says. Kind of like with you and Bess and that old boy."

"Did Alex kill his rival?"

"He threatens to, along about the second verse. Says he's going to stab him, and shoot him with his rifle."

Winston seemed to be thinking about that. He finally said, "Seems a bit much. Maybe he threw in the rifle just to make it rhyme."

"What rhymes with rifle, Winston?"

He was already thinking about that before I said it. I could tell by his smile.

"Wife'll," he said. "You know, like, *My wife'll kill me if she catches me whoring again.*"

We laughed. We clinked bottles and drank.

"And then what happened, Winston?" Doral said. It was like he was waiting for a football to be snapped on a big play.

So I shut up this time. I guessed I wanted to hear what happened next, even more than I wanted the story to just go on forever. Or maybe I realized there's no stopping a story that wants to be told, that needs to be heard.

"And then I thought I heard a little noise," Winston said. "Sounded almost like a breath. Or an owl, off somewhere. Probably just a fish, you know. My own stomach, those ghosts of Moon Lake, some damn thing. A hundred dozen things it could have been, other than that old boy."

"Did you by any means ever check his pulse, Winston?"

"You know, I didn't, brother."

I smiled with him. I couldn't help myself. Or maybe, in that moment, I accepted the complicated world as it was, without the need to understand it, fully, and reduce it to fifteen column inches of black on white. Life is not a newspaper story and life is not a football game; and anyway, if it were, sometimes both teams, the good guys and the bad, would all be suited up in shades of gray. That's what I thought, at least, as I watched Winston's smile fade into something like contentment.

*

"So then you dumped that old boy in the lake, huh, Winston?" Doral said, impatient for his favorite part of the story.
"Yeah, Doral, I did."
"And that old boy probably dead but maybe not."
"I guess you could say."
"So you killed that old boy twice, didn't you, Winston?"
He tousled his little brother's hair.
"Yeah, Doral. Reckon."

*

The next morning, I called a reporter friend at the newspaper. His name was Perkins. He always complained about having to do the work of three people, so we called him Perkins Extended, after the street. He wasn't such a bastard, though. He wasn't too much of a hack.

We exchanged hellos and then he said, "How you hanging in, Charley?"

"I'm, you know, I don't know … still adrift."

He laughed. "Well, that's good. Staying above water, anyway, huh?" He thought he was being nice—the newspaperman version of it.

"They've got you covering night cops now?"

"Hell, that and everything else, seems like. Doing the work of six or seven. Any day now, it might be me delivering your fucking paper in the morning."

"Oh, nah. I cancelled it."

"That's a good man. Can't blame you there. What's up, then?"

"Wondering if you're doing anything on that old boy they pulled out of Moon Lake, week or two ago."

"Bobby Lee DeMent. Yeah, a little. Not much. Moon Lake might as well be the Moon. All we can do to cover Memphis, anymore. But he was local, and a football star way the hell back when. Talked to the cops down that way, couple of days ago. They think it was all to do with a gambling debt. But I think that's just them guessing. Professional job, though. Or anyway, pretty close to one. Semi-pro, I guess you'd say."

"Doesn't sound like they're close to arresting anybody."

"No. Why you asking?"

"Ah, hell, you know. I just miss it, is all."

"The newspaper business?"

"Yeah, I guess. A little."

"Hell of a way to make a living. And more so every day. More so every fucking day. They're talking about another round of cuts. Or we're hearing they're talking. It's the one rumor that's always true."

"The fuckers."

"If I'm lucky it'll be me next. If I'm not, I'll still be here, doing the work of ten or twelve."

"You poor son of a bitch." And then, there being nothing else to say, I said, "Yeah, well, it's good to talk to you, Perk."

"You hang in there, Charley," he said. "Stay adrift."

✳

I woke up the next morning. I went in the kitchen. I made a proper mess of a breakfast. Eggs and sausage and potatoes, and hot sauce on everything like the fucking pox. I ate it and it was good. I put on coffee. I pulled on a hoodie and took a mug outside to drink it. That old Cadillac across the street was gone. It might have been gone for weeks, I don't know.

It was your standard Memphis late-winter day, gray and cold but not to the bone. I drank my coffee. I thought about my old newspaper days. I itched for one to read. I wondered if it was like that phantom limb thing, the feeling you get in the place that isn't there anymore. I really had cancelled it, but more for financial reasons. I'd canceled pretty well everything. I was paying the rent but not much else.

I got down off the porch and walked next door and picked up my neighbor's copy. He never read it, anyway. He'd just toss it in the bin, unopened. I don't know why in hell he still subscribed.

I sat back down, thought maybe I'd open the thing and read about my old friend Winston. Maybe he'd turned himself in, confessed everything. Maybe they hadn't believed him, and he'd taken matters into his own hands, delivered his own sentence, with a gun that actually worked. I'd heard stranger tales. I'd written them.

But no, it was Madison instead.

6

# Funeral day, of all days

He blew his head off. They reported that part in the newspaper. They don't usually, but in this case they had to. He did it out in public, though alone, early hours, in the Old Forest of Overton Park. That was Madison, making news and being a nuisance, a glorious pain in the ass, to the end.

He left a note. Well, Madison's version of one. A thousand words, as ever. His last column.

✳

*They'll say, "Ol' Mad, he was married more times than he could count." OK. So I was bad at math. I'd always been. Love was my thing. I loved them all. I'll love them still, from my cold bed of clay. I'd a great capacity for it, falling in love, being in love. Even in the falling out there were embers among the ashes, and when it's just ashes, is all, cold and gray, dead-seeming, well, where did the fucking Phoenix come from, anyway? Can I say* fucking *in a column now? As an adjective, at least?*

✳

Funeral day. Flippen picked me up.

"It'll be a big turnout, you think?"

"Oh, sure. Even if it's only us and the ex-wives."

We managed to laugh a little.

"What were there, six? Seven?"

"Five, I think. He married the one twice. Lottie, I think it was."

"That was her twice? I thought that was a whole other one."

"She changed her hair, I think. Lost some weight. Glasses."

163

"Son of a bitch. I wonder did Mad realize it?"

We laughed again, for real this time, out loud. And in this way we talked about our deepest feelings, about the death of a friend, and the wheezing gasps of an industry, the threadbare nature of life, the scabs on our own mortality, God and women and how we'd miss Madison, the son of a bitch.

✳

*I never slept with a woman I didn't love. And I never, strictly speaking, cheated. An elucidation, though, if I may: Ongoing relations with multiple ex-wives is not cheating. It's like Lottie said. Or maybe it was Edie. It's gaming the system, at worst. Anyway, they were all in cahoots with me, if not each other. Cahoots is even better than love. Is it not, ladies?*

*Lottie. Audrey. Bobbie Jean. Floozy. Edie. Lottie again.*

*See. I remember.*

*I remember everything.*

✳

Your man in his funeral suit, a faint air of wino about him.

"Hey there, Charley," Vollintine said. "You look good."

"That bad, huh?"

✳

It was a grand funeral. They had it at the Unitarian church, down by the river. Madison's ex-wives got together and voted on it. The Church of the River won, on third ballot, over Earnestine & Hazel's. I think Madison would have preferred the former brothel down on South Main, but it seems a slight majority of the ex-wives still believed in heaven. So a church, it was. One of them, I think it was Floozy, apparently swayed the rest when she said, rather dramatically, "You want to take a trip, you best get yourself to the train station." I wasn't there when she said it, so I

164

don't know if anybody pointed out that Earnestine & Hazel's was just across the street from Central Station.

The minister knew Madison a little—everybody in Memphis, seemed like, knew Madison at least a little. He painted a fair picture of the man. Broad strokes but not bad, for minister's pay. He said Madison's work was his life and his life's work was to champion the common man. He said Madison had a big heart and a finely honed sense of outrage and that he did, in his way, what some would call God's work. He said Madison was not, by any account, a spiritual man, or a believer in a higher being, but that he was on the right side of things. "He was a great man, in this way," the minister said, "even if, by his own accounts and those of his, well, several former wives, he sometimes struggled with being a good one. Now he's gone. We'll miss him. I dare say many of you already do."

✳

*I boxed, in my youth. A wicked belt of a left, I had, but a chin like a Tiffany bud vase. I don't mean just delicate, but outright pretty. A beaut. I was proud of it, too. I'd drop the gloves and preen for the crowd. It's how I got my ring nickname, thanks to some old cut man:* Proverbs 16:18. *Look it up. Would have been a hell of a thing to have stitched onto your satin robe and have to explain. It's why I went into the newspaper game, where I could preen sitting down. I still got hit sometimes, on account of what I wrote. But I loved it, sitting down and bashing those keys, banging out those columns, bringing those crooks and fat cats down, down, down.*

✳

The minister asked if anyone wanted to speak. A small procession of us trudged up to the pulpit. Flippen said Madison just loved a good story, above all else. That's what drove him. He said it was like Furry Lewis, the old Memphis blues singer, who used to sing about how he had nineteen women and wanted just one more. Flippen said, "Furry, he sang about how if the one was good he'd let the nineteen go. Well, Madison was like that with stories." Flippen grinned then. He looked down on the front row at all those ex-wives. "Well, son of a bitch. I guess he was like that with women, too." It was good to hear a flock of grieving widows laugh out loud, full-throated, there in a church, on funeral day, of all days.

✳

*I'd rather write columns than fuck, but it was close.*

✳

Stell was next. She said everybody who read Madison in the newspapers had a treat, but the real joy was to drink with the man, to hear those stories told live. She said Madison was nothing shy of jazz. She said he was a wild, after-hours session. "His voice like a thud, a rumble," she said, and then, because she was Stell, because she couldn't help being Stell, she said, "It was not for nothing the old son of a bitch was the size and shape of an old bull fiddle."

It was pretty much my life's ambition to never have to stand up and speak to a crowd, but I wanted to, this time. I needed to. Then I saw Pearl starting to stand, and I did, too. So we did a little impromptu duet. We weren't bad, for funeral entertainment. I said Madison was the best of us, a bulldog reporter who wrote like an Irish poet. Pearl said he drank like one, too. (Don't forget to tip your pallbearers.) I said he had the greatest capacity for outrage, and whiskey, of any man I'd ever seen, that he was one of the few windbags whose company I enjoyed. I said that while the rest of us were trying to tell the truth, and tripping over our own feet patting ourselves on the back for it, Madison was out there going us one better. I said the lot of us wrote stories that were strictly true or essentially true, the legal definition of truth as it pleases the court. But Mad didn't chase the truth. He had a higher aim. He wrote an *honest* column. I said it was an accomplishment on par with man setting foot on the moon, or maybe that record Duke Ellington made with Charles Mingus, and Madison did it three times a week for more years than I could remember. Pearl said, "I'd never have said this while the man was alive, you know, but here's the truth: I took pictures. That son of a bitch painted them."

I don't know how many times the words "son of a bitch" were uttered that day from the church sanctuary, but those who bet the over were drinking the good stuff that night.

When the applause died down, I said, "Oh, and one note, to those of you who thought he made up Lauderdale Slim, the rag-and-bone man. Well, he didn't. I met the man this morning. There he is, back row, in the gray tweed suit. Looking sharp, Slim. Looking natty."

He nodded back as heads turned to see him.

"Condolences on the loss of your good friend and shotgun rider," I said. "Condolences to us all. And to God, or Scratch, who must deal with the great man now."

✳

*I'd rather fuck than cure cancer. I'm a little chagrined to say it but only a little. Points for honesty, eh, God?*

✳

Stell and I hugged outside. She said I looked like shit, but that I'd said some good words.

"You, too, Stell. You, too. The words, I mean."

"How are you getting on, Charley?"

"Well, I don't think I'll throw myself off one of the railroad bridges, if that's what you mean. It seems, I don't know, unnecessary, after all this."

"Madison died for your sins, eh?"

"Something like that."

They buried him in Memorial Park Cemetery, another drinking buddy for Charlie Rich.

The minister said a few final words and then said we were all invited to the home of Madison's ex-wife Edie. She was unique in the flock—the closest thing to what you'd call a proper lady. Not even East Memphis matrons were immune to Madison's charms, I guessed.

She lived on Shady Grove. It was a catered affair. I stood on the wraparound porch, drinking bourbon and holding a plate of funeral food. It was meat of some sort, under a glaze of something else, with various stalks and pellets scattered meticulously about it, in what I believe they call "presentation."

I was out there with Lauderdale Slim. I'd gotten a ride over with him. He drove his old white truck. I started to give him directions, but he said he knew the neighborhood, from his R&B rounds. He said he once picked up a 1959 Triumph Bonneville motorcycle from a house down the street. He said it had a note taped to it that said, "Take this, please, before my damn fool husband kills himself on it." Slim said he sold the thing for more money than he'd made in some entire years.

"I might want to ride with you some day, if you don't mind."

"You on the lookout for a motorcycle, Charley Hull? You wanna go and get your damn fool self killed?"

"A typewriter," I said.

He sniffed at something on his plate, took a bite. He smiled, and then washed it down with a good swig of bourbon.

"Way Mad used to talk, you safer off with a motorcycle," he said.

Stell came up behind me, reached around and snapped up a piece of meat off my plate. She scrunched her face as she ate it, then she smiled. The fuck were they serving, Happy Meals?

"Hmm," she said.

"What is it?"

"Besides holy-shit good? Be damned if I know."

"I could go for a Tops burger."

Slim said, "I don't know, Charley. Tastes pretty damned good." He took another bite. He seemed to be thinking about it. He smiled. "Don't y'all tell my dead mama, but this the best damned succotash I ever tasted."

"You've been spending too much time in these fancy neighborhoods, Slim," I said.

"Hell, Charley. You got to go where the good shit is. Rag-and-bone man rule, No. 1. My dead daddy told me that."

I took a bite. Well, fuck me.

✳

It was a grand party. There was much eating and drinking, and stories were told. Madison's greatest hits. My favorite was the time the ex-mayor died and one of the local TV stations interviewed Madison, his nemesis, outside the church. The reporter asked why Madison had come to the funeral of a man who'd sued him twice over his columns and called for his firing dozens of times.

"To make sure," Mad said to the camera, steeple rising over his left shoulder.

Then someone began playing the piano, drawing the drunken mourners around. I didn't know the piano player, but he wasn't bad. He played old jazz, Madison's music. He played rags and drags, then he slowed it way down. A couple of Mad's ex-wives sang. They weren't bad, either. Songbirds of the barfly variety, holding high that torch they all carried for Madison, passing it around. They sang "Crazy He Calls Me" and "My Old Flame" and "He's Funny That Way."

Only the bull fiddle was missing.

✳

Later, I was walking up Shady Grove toward Wick and Emily's house. I must have been a sight, for any East Memphis matrons looking out their windows—a one-man funeral procession in want of another funeral, a drum major wino sot with shirt-tail half out, suit coat slung over my shoulder. But I wasn't drunk, really. I believe I'd drunk myself sober. Take that, science. Fuck you.

A car stopped. The driver rolled down the window. I didn't recognize her face, but the voice took me back.

"Well, if it's not Mr. Truth and Honesty."

*

"I'm sorry about your friend."

"It's you."

"From that day in the bookstore, yeah. We bickered. I won." She gave me her hand to shake. "I'm Fay."

"I'm Charley. Did you know him?"

"Madison? Only from the funny papers, as they say. He might have come in the restaurant sometime. One of my servers said so."

"You're—you."

"Huh? Oh, yeah. Like I said. Fay. Fay Cook. I saw you inside a couple of times but you had your head down, so I just let you be. I didn't know if it was grief or, you know, you stare at your shoes a lot. I was busy, anyway. My restaurant—we catered the thing for your friend. I never know what to call these ... things."

"After-party?" I smiled. "Madison wouldn't have minded. Only that he missed it. Your daughter, she's dating Jimmy Ricketts?"

"You didn't hear? They're engaged. Sweet boy, but I've begged her not to take his name. Tilly Ricketts—sounds like the dirty bits in a sea shanty. *Then she pulled up her dress way up high, and she showed him her ...*"

I laughed. I said, "I worked with Jimmy. They let us go at the same time."

"I know. He's doing great, by the way. He's taken right to advertising. A natural, apparently."

"I'm sorry to hear that." I tried not to sound like too much of an asshole.

"Yeah, Tilly says you thought Jimmy was a born newspaperman and couldn't face life after. Did you really think he'd jump off one of the railroad bridges?"

"I was—"

"Projecting?"

"Concerned, I'd like to think."

"Well, anyway," she said, "can I give you ride home? You don't live around here, I don't guess."

I was standing outside her car, in the middle of Shady Grove. I said, "My friends, they live down here a ways. The Carrs."

"Wick and Emily? Oh, they're lovely. They come in the restaurant. They'll eat anything I can dream up and give some silly, crackpot name to. Get in, I'll drop you there."

"OK, then."

Wick and Emily weren't home, so she offered to take me to my place. I said I didn't want to be a bother. She asked where I lived and I told her. She said it wasn't a bother, that she could drop me off on her way back to the restaurant. It opened for dinner in few hours. I said, "Well, if it's no bother."

"Quit going on about it being such a bloody bother before you become one. Get in, you."

She was bossy. I liked that. I got in. We didn't talk, not much. She had the radio tuned to WEVL, the local volunteer station, playing "Starkville City Jail," by Johnny Cash, from his *At San Quentin* album. Johnny wrote it after getting himself arrested in Starkville, Mississippi, at three in the morning for picking flowers. I told this story to Fay as she drove. She smiled as she listened.

"Picking flowers," she said, turning left off Union to Cooper. "Was that some kind of hophead slang for getting potted?"

I laughed. I looked at her. She was dark-haired and had it curled around her ear. She was flinty-eyed. She had a strong profile, would have looked good on a quarter. Three songs for your smile, Ms. Cook. Or sort-of smile—her mouth had a hint of a rumor of a curl to it, as if she was on the verge of some retort.

She drove like a woman with six things to do yet, but five could wait. She was a grown woman, a pistol, she used words like "hophead" and "funny papers" and "crackpot." She could have been in a gumshoe movie with Humphrey Bogart in 1946 instead of driving my ass home like I was some kind of overgrown runaway from the State Home for Children of Dubious Origins.

"Hey, I just thought of something," I said. "You're a chef named Cook."

"That's not the half of it."

"What's the rest?"

"My mother always claimed we were related to Annie Cook. You know, Madame Annie."

I knew. She was famous, if you knew your Memphis history—how she turned her fancy brothel, the Mansion House, into a hospital for the yellow fever victims of the 1870s. She eventually caught the fever herself and died, and is buried in Elmwood Cemetery with a big headstone that calls her "A Nineteenth Century Mary Magdelene." Yep, they misspelled Magdalene. Also, strictly speaking, I believe the whole Mags-was-a-prostitute thing has been debunked. So even stonemasons need copy editors. Or especially stonemasons.

"Is it true?"

"Almost certainly not, though I didn't tell my mother that. She was so in love with the idea—what a life, Madame Annie; what a place, the Mansion House. Anyway, Annie's people were from Germany and ours from Ireland."

"Ah, Ireland. One of my favorite places on earth. You been?"

"Top of my to-do list," she said. "Just waiting for the right drinking buddy to go with."

She drove on. She only about got us killed twice more. We were almost to my place now.

"Look," I said. "This is going to be a funny kind of thing to say, but I'm glad I was such an asshole that day in the bookstore."

"Because otherwise I wouldn't have talked to you?"

"Yeah."

"You don't know that. I talk to strangers all the time. I'm in the restaurant business. I never met a stranger."

"I was a bit strange."

"In your bathrobe, yeah. And slippers. Poor bastard."

She threw her head back and laughed. I laughed, too—with her, at me, at life, and hard times, the whole smear.

Then we were outside my house. I got out and then leaned in the window, like I had something to say. I thought something would come to me. I thought I might be, for the approximately the first time in my life, suave or glib. Instead I just stared at her. She stared back, smiling. She seemed to like watching me suffer there. I thought she might finally say something, save me, but that hint of a rumor of a curl was unfounded. Never fall for a rumor—an old newspaper man told me that. ("Or a woman who can out-drink you," was the rest of that advice.)

So it was down to me to say something. So I did. I said, "Your succotash is amazing." I don't think Bogie ever put it that way to Bacall, but then I didn't have to worry about the Hays Code.

I stepped back from the car and looked down at my funeral shoes. So I couldn't see her smiling as she pulled away; I just knew that she was.

"You men and your hophead slang," she said.

# The bottom-feeding fellow

We started spending time together, when we could. One of us was working hard enough for two and the other had started looking again for a job. We'd meet for a few minutes on the stoop out back of her restaurant, drink coffee and talk. Her restaurant was a short drive from my house, so it was nothing to come over, when I didn't have an interview for some high-powered position or other, mind you.

On days when we had some time, we'd take long drives out into the sticks in search of catfish. She was on an eternal search for interesting things to do in the kitchen with the bottom-feeding fellow. I said it was like putting spats on a dog. I said to let him be, he was fine just as God and some Alabama catfish farmer made him. She said I was a bit of a bottom feeder myself. Well, she had me there.

We saw Dylan play the Orpheum. He wore a cowboy suit and croaked through his songs and it was grand. He looked like a cross between Snidely Whiplash, The Joker, and some finely whiskered catfish. He didn't call me up on stage to sing "It Takes a Lot to Laugh, It Takes a Train to Cry." He didn't play that song at all, but he did play her favorite of his, "You Ain't Goin' Nowhere." I love that one, too, said it was my seventh-favorite Dylan song of all time. She said, "You have, like, actual rankings." I said I did. I said they're updated on a fairly regular basis. She said it must be a man thing. I said it was a boy thing that men kept going when they grew up.

"How would you rank me?"

"Nonpareil."

"Like the little chocolate candy with sprinkles?"

"No," I said, smiling, scrambling—my permanent condition, seemed like, in her presence. "Like Thomas Hart Benton's 'Achelous and Hercules,' and the fight scene in 'The Quiet Man,' and the tamales at Fat Mama's in Natchez."

"Thanks, I think. I thought you were trying to get me in bed before the tamale bit." And then: "Fat Mama's, huh? If they're as good as Doe's in Greenville, I need to take a road trip."

We bickered some, too—that was best of all. We bickered over which barbecue joint had the best shoulder and whether shoulder was better chopped or pulled. We bickered over whose ribs were best dry and whose were best wet, and whether there should be a third category, since some ribs deemed wet were really more glazed, like at Corky's, while others were sopping with sauce, like at Interstate.

And back to our bickery, if that's a word. I wanted nothing but earth tones on my plate. She said I ate like a fourth-grader. There was a new restaurant downtown that she liked, called (holler)—with those parentheses, lower-cased—where you apparently could get neckbones served on china plates, with cloth napkins, and pay twenty dollars for the privilege. She said I was just trying to keep the neckbones down. She called me a bottom feeder. I shouted, "Channel cat! Blue! Flathead!"

Mondays were best. Her restaurant was closed. We'd drive to Pickwick or Shiloh, or down to Greenville, in Mississippi, for tamales at Doe's Eat Place, or just nowhere at all. Or we'd go to the record store, load up on old soul albums and go to my place or hers, listen to them for hours in bed. Sometimes, I'd cook for her, dishes with fanciful names, schmancy names, and grand back stories, but it was always just a grilled cheese sandwich.

Some nights, late, after the restaurant was closed, she'd call. She'd talk about her day. She'd talk about her aching feet and other pains. She'd say I was a good listener. I'd say I ought to be, I used to do it professionally.

One night, tired of talking, she said, "Play me a record, Charley. Let's just listen to it, the both of us, here on the phone."

"What'll it be?"

"Oh, you know, something old, with horns and gypsy violins, double and triple entendres. Some of those old dirty blues. Fuck, I don't know."

"The mouth on you, Ms. Cook."

"Well, get over here and kiss it."

✳

"Our Charley's in love, Wick."

"Oh, a little," I said to Emily.

We were having a picnic, the four of us and baby Jesse C., too. It was a Memphis kind of thing. We were down the bluff a little, in the shadow of the old railroad bridges, down where Emily and I had gone looking for Jimmy Ricketts, all those months ago. It looked more than ever like a drug drop, or some hobo picnic ground. It was perfect. It was spring.

"Can you be just a little in love, Wick?"

"Oh, I wouldn't know, Em."

Fay had gone back to the car for some utensil or something. We were having all manner of food she'd made. She'd done some perfectly absurd things with catfish and I would have admitted, under threat of lashing, that they were damned tasty and perhaps had taken the old bottom-feeding fellow to a good and higher place.

"Smart man," Emily said to me. "It's why I married him. That, and I was a little in love."

"I thought you married me for my money," Wick said, "and my boyish good looks."

Fay was back. She said, "You two," to Wick and Emily. She reached for little Jesse C. She hoisted up the little thing. He was a fine one. He was several months old now and had given up the saxophone wail, for the most part. He had some of Wick's boyish good looks. I saw Emily in him, too. He was a green-eyed prize.

We ate and drank and talked. Wick said he had a client who was a state rep and a closet atheist who wanted to come out. We asked him what he advised the godless fellow. Wick said, "I told him not to." And? "He didn't." I said, "And they pay you for that?" "They do." Wick looked sheepish when he said it, showing those boyish good looks to fine effect.

176

Emily said she'd started a suite of poems based on the Mississippi Delta blues. She said she was deep now into the long and crucial middle section, which concerned itself mostly with sex. She said the blues women, though there weren't as many, were as dirty as the men. She said what might be the dirtiest blues ever, "Shave 'Em Dry," was by a woman, Lucille Bogan. She said Memphis Minnie, who could play guitar as good as any man, who beat Big Bill Broonzy in a cutting contest one night up in Chicago, had all manner of suggestive songs. Emily sang a little of Minnie's song about her ice man.

Fay was still holding the baby. I reached over and covered the chap's ears. Jesse Charles gave out a little coo then. Along with Wick's boyish good looks, he had Emily's perfect timing.

Fay said she had some investors who wanted her to open a second restaurant, but all she wanted to do was lose herself in the kitchen, the cooking. She said whenever she had to think about the actual business part, she wanted to reach for a cleaver and take it all out on some poor bird or critter.

"Shave 'em dry!" I shouted. "Cutting contest! Club Neckbone!"

They laughed, and then Wick, as I knew he would, saw through the diversion.

"So how's your, um, search for honest work going, Charley?"

"I'm trying," I said. "I had another interview. I'd write press releases."

"You could do that in your sleep."

"That doesn't sound much like fun. I like to sleep in my sleep. I like to dream."

"What do you dream about, Charley?" This was Emily.

"Oh, dragons and sea beasts, you know, and me, doing battle with the things. Lots of derring-do and sword play. Trying to save a damsel who seems to be fine as she is. She's wearing a dragon-tooth necklace and frying up some sea-beast croquettes."

And then they all pretty much said, at pretty much the same time, "But what do you want to *do*, Charley?"

So I told them.

"I want to find steady work I don't detest. I want to make a little scratch, not much. I want to re-up my newspaper subscription, if they're still putting one out, and buy a new used car. I want to take banjo lessons, get a dog, try to read *Remembrance of Things Past*. Really. And I want to be a more adventurous eater. Not really. I want to be, if it's not asking too much, cool—to feel what that must feel like, comfortable in my bones, clothes draping off me, like Bogie or John Lee Hooker, or hell, you, Wick. Cool—but just for a day. Cool for a day, like a contest you could win. And I want, most of all, and even if it's a bother, to marry Ms. Fay Cook. I want to be her kitchen man. I want to wash some dishes, get my hands wet and sudsy in some manual labor. I want to be just a wee bit more of a people person, but only a wee bit—chat up some strangers, tell the odd joke. I want to write, honestly, truthfully, about my life, whether anybody wants to read it or not. Oh, and I'd like another of those catfish things."

And so, with the help of my friends, something of a plan was hatched.

# Sweet Friday

And then we had the reception. It was lovely with love and happiness, as in the old soul song by the Reverend Al Green. No one cried. Well, only a little. We all cried a little, it's true, but joyfully so. We chased tears with stronger stuff. We shouted over the sound of the band. We danced and sang along, and may have cried again, happy tears, for we were, in the end, so very, very drunk.

I remember it all. It began with a speech. It was your man who gave it. I said we live in a world of doom and joy and all that's between. Just walking out the front door in the morning is chancy, I said. Fate crouches in the flower beds and up trees and down alleys. You have to mind yourself out there. But out there, I said, that's where the treasures are. That's where the stories are. That's where life is.

I remember dancing with Fay, mother of the bride. Her daughter Tilly had taken Jimmy Ricketts to be her lawfully wedded (but she hadn't taken his name, smart girl). They were dancing, too. They were a lovely married couple, and we weren't half bad ourselves. We'd gotten ourselves quietly hitched a few weeks before. I'd moved into her house in Cooper-Young, but we were looking for something downtown. Tilly and Jimmy would move into her mom's house. As for my Midtown bungalow, it was a historical site now, tours given and all, of the rooms where the last living newspaperman, poor bastard, had written on the walls his possible new careers, lines from novels he'd never write, and the like. Nah, just fucking with you. It was scrubbed clean and repainted and rented to some new tenants who didn't know or care about its sordid past.

✳

And I remember telling Fay I loved her—"flat feet and all," I said, "flat feet and all"—but she couldn't hear me for the band.

They were raising a fine and proper ruckus. It was the Church Keys—our young friend's gal had come back, against considerable odds, after a year or more in New Orleans. The music, culture, and lore of the Crescent City had as much influence on her as the Bluff City's had on him, in their time apart. When they got the band back together, they added a rhythm section and horns, fashioned a new sound from found parts. There were elements of ragtime and jump blues, the funky penguin and the ooh, poo, pah doo. They still played some of the old songs, but done in all manner of different styles. Their songs had steam and tail feathers, they had froth and kick. They even played a couple of different versions of "Hard Times." In my favorite of the two, it sounded like Hard Times had won the lottery, or at least found purpose and steady work …

*

This was all back down on old South Main, where began this mostly true and sorely honest tale. It was something like sixteen months, six days, three hours, a couple of thousand beers, five hundred-some bourbons (neat), untold little humiliations, and a handful of outright near-life experiences since I was sacked by the daily rag. ("If it had only been the cancer, instead of a paper cut …" said one of the old hacks.)

The city declared Wick's property a "Dangerous/Derelict" building, not long after he bought it. They stapled a notice to the plywood, over a buffalo's haunch. And so Dixie-fried Narnia could be no more. The woods were cut down, the jungle hacked to the ground, and construction began. A building rose from the stubble—a large main floor and two half floors above, overlooking it. There was brick and stone and steel, and big windows. We still didn't know what the place would become, but it took shape, over long sessions of drink and gab and jukebox hymns. There was much debate and many wild-hair notions, the wildest of which tended to prevail. In the end it became a restaurant, and we'd rent it out for events, too—Winston's little brother Doral and his pugilist bride had their reception there. Winston, locked up and awaiting trial, sent his best wishes. He'd turned himself in, confessed everything, once Angel accepted Doral's proposal. He'd told me Doral didn't need a father figure anymore, now that he'd have a wife who could kick anyone's ass—and his own new personal sports hero in the bargain.

We called the restaurant Sup, a place without pretense—or arugula. I wanted to call it Hard Times, after my favorite song and personal anthem; they wouldn't let me. But if you scan the lyrics you'll notice the word "sup," as in "Let us pause in life's pleasures and count its many tears / While we all sup sorrow with the poor," so there, take that. Plus, in another lyrical nod to Mr. Foster's famed number, there was a sign over the door as you left, saying "Come Again No More." Wick said it didn't seem like much of a business strategy, but I insisted. And the food? Oh, it was a little fancy for my taste, mind you. But nobody told Fay Cook-Hull what to serve.

The kitchen was hers—we'd talked her into a second restaurant, somehow. I roamed all about the place, a man with three jobs. But then, I'd asked for them, every one. I had them printed on my business card, as much to remind me as anything. I was bartender and chief bottle washer and writer-in-residence. I needed, I decided, to be another two-thirds humbled, even after sixteen months as a shiftless ex-wag.

Bartending taught me to be a more social person, to talk to strangers, make friends, dispense drinks and wisdom as such was sought, to spring the odd quip or whimsy. Mostly, I found, people needed you to listen, and then tell them that yes, life was a wicked bitch of a bastard whore, but with perseverance and refreshments it could generally be survived. I know, I know; I was getting inspirational in my middle age …

Washing dishes was work. That's all the hell it was. It was not exalting and did not bring me nearer to the soul of anything. But it was honest toil, and that's what I needed, to roll up my sleeves and switch off my mind and do the small thing that needed to be done. It was a bit of a revelation, even so: All those years, I'd thought those glasses cleaned themselves …

✳

The mornings were mine. I wrote in the mornings. It was just me, up on that half of a third floor, looking down on the quiet emptiness below. I could hear old South Main starting to stir. Car horns and the slow rumble of a trolley, occasionally a fire truck from Station No. 2, out on an early call.

Coffee. Writing. Some old songs on the box.

I wrote on an old Underwood, a teacher's model with no letters on the keys. I bought it off Lauderdale Slim. He claimed it had been used by Shelby Foote to write those books about the Civil War, in his big house over on East Parkway. I seemed to recall Mr. Foote wrote with dip pens and said he wanted nothing mechanical between himself and the page. But it was a good story, even if it did add ten dollars to the purchase price.

I wasn't much of a typist, still just a two-finger banger. Fingers struck keys and the typebar snapped-to and letters appeared on the page and letters formed words and words fancied themselves as sentences. On the good days, anyway. Other days, bad days, the words were elusive sons of bitches and I didn't get so much as a sentence down. But at least I knew the story. It was mine.

✳

It's a hell of a thing, you know, to wake up knowing that *Sweet Thursday* has already been written. But what are you going to do, jump off the railroad bridge on that account? Maybe I'd write about Friday instead. Always was fond of that day.

✳

182

"Is it true, Charley? Is it honest? Your book. Is it the flaming shit-bag of lies I know you have in you?" Fay would say.

✳

I pecked and banged. I worked my way, wrote my way, slowly to that day, the day in the Delta with Emily, when we raced and she won. I wended my way there. I wore shoes this time. I made myself just slightly faster afoot, but still not so much that I won. I had to lose, or else it might have been me who found the gun. I wouldn't have had the piss and gumption to pick it up—even now, in the retelling—much less point it at another soul, and least of all my beloved thirteen-year-old girl cuz.

So we raced and she won and then we were in the woods. She held the gun. It was as cheap-looking and mud-crusted as ever. She double-fisted the thing. She pointed it at my feet …

✳

That's as far as I got today. Time now to tend bar and wash dishes. Honest work to do.

It's Friday, and a sweet one, at that. I don't write on the weekends. So I'll take up the story again Monday morning. I'll ponder it over the weekend, but I think I know how it'll go.

Emily will point that pistol at my feet. She'll say those same words she said that day, all those years ago and all over again. The damned thing may well fire this time, I don't know, can't yet say. But no matter. I'll be dancing this time.

# About the Author

David Wesley Williams, a native Kentuckian now living in Memphis, Tennessee, is the author of the novels *Everybody Knows* and *Long Gone Daddies*. His short fiction has been published by the *Oxford American*, *Kenyon Review Online*, and such literary journals as *The Common* and *The Pinch*. He spent thirty-five years as a newspaper reporter and editor, covering Olympic Games, the aftermath of Hurricane Katrina, and much in between.

# Acknowledgment

The opening portion of this novel originally appeared in somewhat different form as "The Newspaper Wake" in *Kenyon Review Online* (2020).

V. Joshua Adams * Mark Baumgartner * Scott Shibuya Brown * Michael Chin * Chloe Clark * Rivka Clifton * Brittney Corrigan * Jessica Cuello * Barbara Cully * Allison Cundiff * Curious Theatre Branch * Neil de la Flor * Genevieve DeGuzman * Suzanne Frischkorn * Victoria Garza * Reginald Gibbons * Joachim Glage * Caroline Goodwin * Brett Hanley * Kathryn Kruse * Brigitte Lewis * Jenny Magnus * DK McCutchen * Jean McGarry * Rita Mookerjee * Mamie Morgan * Alexis Orgera * Zach Powers * Karen Rigby * Jo Salas * Maureen Seaton * Kristine Snodgrass * Cornelia Spelman * Peter Stenson * Melissa Studdard * Gemini Wahhaj * Megan Weiler * David Welch * Cassandra Whitaker * David Wesley Williams

jacklegpress.org